An LAPD lieutenant named Johnny Gomez was in charge of this part of the police line. He had 250 cops under his direct command, all of them trained in riot tactics and crowd control, all of them stretched twenty feet in front of him, suddenly battling furiously with the onrushing demonstrators. This was not good. Gomez and his men had been preparing for this day for weeks, but again, that training had been based on what had happened at past anti-WTO demonstrations: rocks, bottles, maybe a Molotov Cocktail or two, with moderate property damage to nearby stores, and a constant ripple up and down the police line, but never any concerted attempts to break through.

What Gomez was looking at now—a concentrated, almost pinpoint assault on a small part of the overall line—hadn't been covered in the training.

"This isn't how it's supposed to go!" he cried, as his men buckled further.

That's when a second, even more concentrated wave of protesters hit the police line. Gomez saw them coming. There were maybe a hundred or so, again many armed with baseball bats and rebar. But to his horror, Gomez saw some of the demonstrators carrying something else: AK-47 assault rifles.

Books by Jack Shane

Sky Hunters
ANARCHY'S REIGN
OPERATION SOUTHERN CROSS
X-BATTALION

ATTENTION: ORGANIZATIONS AND CORPORATIONS
Most Harper paperbacks are available at special quantity discounts for bulk purchases for sales promotions, premiums, or fund raising. For information, please call or write:

**Special Markets Department, HarperCollins Publishers,
10 East 53rd Street, New York, New York 10022-5299.
Telephone: (212) 207-7528.   Fax: (212) 207-7222.**

SKY HUNTERS
ANARCHY'S REIGN

JACK SHANE

HARPER
An Imprint of HarperCollins*Publishers*

This is a work of fiction. Names, characters, places, and incidents are products of the author's imagination or are used fictitiously and are not to be construed as real. Any resemblance to actual events, locales, organizations, or persons, living or dead, is entirely coincidental.

HARPER

An Imprint of HarperCollins*Publishers*
195 Broadway
New York, NY, 10007

Copyright © 2007 by Jack Shane
ISBN: 978-0-06-073243-1
ISBN-10: 0-06-073243-1

All rights reserved. No part of this book may be used or reproduced in any manner whatsoever without written permission, except in the case of brief quotations embodied in critical articles and reviews. For information address Harper paperbacks, an imprint of HarperCollins Publishers.

First Harper paperback printing: January 2007

HarperCollins® and Harper® are registered trademarks of HarperCollins Publishers.

Printed in the United States of America

Visit Harper paperbacks on the World Wide Web at www.harpercollins.com

10 9 8 7 6 5 4 3 2

If you purchased this book without a cover, you should be aware that this book is stolen property. It was reported as "unsold and destroyed" to the publisher, and neither the author nor the publisher has received any payment for this "stripped book."

For my good friend,
Scooter

SKY HUNTERS

ANARCHY'S REIGN

PART ONE

CHAPTER 1

THE FREAK STORM HAD BEEN BATTERING THE PACIFIC
coastline for six days.

It had made a mess of things in southern California.
Streets washed-out in Beverly Hills, heavy flooding in
the Valley, mudslides near Malibu. Large sections of Los
Angeles County had lost power. Phone service was out
too. Tsunami-sized waves had even chased the surfers
away from La Jolla and Ventura Beach.

The storm was far worse out at sea. The winds were
blowing at hurricane force fifty miles offshore. The rain
was coming down in sheets, and waves as high as forty
feet had been reported. Most Pacific gales blew themselves out in a day or two, but not this one. It seemed
like it would go on forever.

All this meant the U.S. Coast Guard had been busy all
week. Its main station in southern California was located
just north of San Diego at Los Quinos Point. All of its rescue boats were at sea, working overtime. Their mission: to

get to vessels radioing for help and locate those that were missing. They'd been at it nearly 150 hours straight.

The Los Quinos station had sixteen rescue boats. Fifteen were RHIs, sixteen-foot fast boats used for rescues within 20 miles of land. The remaining boat was a 270-foot, medium endurance cutter, CGS *Steadfast*. Built to operate for weeks at a time at sea, when storms came across the Pacific and hung around like this one, the *Steadfast* could easily wind up rescuing dozens of people. Pleasure boaters, fishermen, crews of small freighters, souls out beyond the horizon who would have been lost otherwise.

The *Steadfast* had been at sea since the storm began. Moving up and down the coastline about seventy-five miles out, its crew had rescued twenty-six people in that time. These survivors were huddled in the ship's mess hall—safe, but forced to endure the same stomach-churning conditions as the crew. The weather was so bad, all Coast Guard helicopters had been grounded, so the civilians could not be taken off, not just yet.

And as the *Steadfast* would remain out here for as long as the Coast Guard kept receiving SOS calls, the rescued boaters still had some uncomfortable hours ahead of them.

IT WAS AROUND MIDNIGHT, THE START OF THE *STEAD- *fast*'s seventh day at sea, when strange things began to happen.

The cutter's radio team suddenly found their equipment besieged by a massive cloud of electronic interference. The radiomen were experts; they'd experienced problems caused by static before. They knew unstable atmospheric conditions could wreak havoc on modern communications equipment. But they'd never seen anything like this.

The radio room reported the bizarre disturbance to the ship's communications officer. He ordered them to filter out the interference as best they could, as there might be SOS calls hidden within. Meanwhile, outside, the cutter was battling thirty-foot waves and 60 knot winds. The sea was so violent it caused the ship's lights to flicker crazily. Weird shadows were being cast all over the ship. The exhausted crewmen were nearing their breaking point.

It took the ship's radiomen ten minutes to get their communication sets back to something resembling normal. With about half the clutter cleared away, they were able to once again concentrate on the emergency maritime frequencies, radio bands that anyone in trouble out here would use when calling for help.

And yes, as soon as they could hear again, they detected radio chatter on the main emergency band. Many voices, all speaking at once. *So* many, it was hard to tell what anyone was saying. The radiomen battled to isolate each voice, bringing everything down to basics, and after a while some individual conversations could be heard. More important, the location of where the voices were coming from could also be determined.

But right away the radiomen knew something was wrong. The cutter's surface radar team was telling them two mid-sized cargo ships were within a mile of the *Steadfast*—and that the explosion of radio chatter was coming from these two vessels alone. Yet, even though there was a lot of conversation going on between the two cargo ships, the discussion was not about their vessels being in trouble—Mayday calls and such. Rather, the chatter was about transferring some very precious cargo from one ship to another.

The two ships were only 1,500 yards away, in the thick in the storm like the *Steadfast*. Even a large cargo ship would be in danger in these circumstances. Why were these guys talking about moving cargo back and forth in the middle of this tempest? It didn't make sense.

The *Steadfast*'s captain was briefed on the situation. He immediately turned the cutter toward the two ships. The wind had picked up to 70 knots, and the seas were growing by the second. The rain was so fierce the *Steadfast* was forced to steer via its sea-surface radar. This was as rough as any of the crew had seen it. For the rescued boaters below, it was pure hell.

Even at full speed, it took the *Steadfast* more than fifteen minutes to reach the two ships. Attempts to contact them along the way had been fruitless. The cutter's home base at Los Quinos Point was now aware of the situation. But all they could do was wait until the cutter made visual contact with the two freighters. Only then would they know whether the ships were in danger or not.

Finally, those on the cutter's bridge could see faint lights ahead of them. The sea-surface radar confirmed first one, then two ships looming off their port bow. Astonishingly, a smaller vessel, a launch of some kind, could be seen battling the waves, moving between the two ships.

This confirmed the intercepted conversations. The two vessels were indeed transferring something—or someone—from one to the other. But this was also insanity—the waves were topping thirty-two feet, the wind was now up to 85 miles an hour. It seemed as if the smaller boat would be swept away at any moment. But it got even stranger. Still monitoring the ships' communications, the cutter's radio team could tell this wasn't a rescue operation in progress—that had been the only reasonable explanation for such foolhardiness. No, these conversations, spoken in garbled English, were way out of whack. Instead of people screaming Mayday, SOS, and so on, there was swearing, cursing, and arguing going on. All of it appeared to be centered on the small boat moving from one ship to the other, and the radiomen thought they could hear the names "Douglas" and "Jerome" interjected over and over again.

Finally the cutter's bridge crew saw both ships in profile. They *were* freighters, about the same size, maybe 20,000 tons each. They were very rusty, and not flying any flags that they could see. The captain called down to his radiomen and told them to reach someone on either ship via any channel necessary. That the people were arguing over sea lane emergency channels wasn't just outlandish, it was also against international law. At the very least it showed a woefully amateurish approach to ocean travel.

The *Steadfast* closed to within a hundred yards of the two ships. The cutter's radiomen engaged their in-close, emergency channel override system, allowing them to break into the two ships' on-board communications. This silenced all the chatter between the two freighters. With the channel now clear, the radiomen requested that the ships identify themselves and asked if they needed assistance. More than a dozen times they sent out this message.

But there was no reply.

BACK AT THE COAST GUARD BASE AT LOS QUINOS Point, the station's senior officers were gathered around the facility's communication hub, listening intently to the strange drama playing out seventy-five miles away. The officers had ordered the station's main and backup tape recorders to capture the audio feed of what was going on. Even some of the enlisted men were standing nearby, listening in.

They were all tuned in to the *Steadfast*'s bridge communications; they could clearly hear the captain giving orders to his crew. But just a few seconds after the cutter's radiomen had finally barged in on the off-color chatter between the two storm-tossed ships, everything suddenly went quiet. Even the noise of the howling storm disappeared. What was heard next shook everyone listening in: a loud bang, followed by cries coming from the cutter's bridge. Then another bang, this one twice as loud, twice as violent. More cries from the *Steadfast*'s crew.

Then the cutter's captain was heard crying out: *"What the hell is that?"*

After that, there was silence.

CHAPTER 2

THE SQUADRON OF ABRAMS M1-A1 TANKS RACED across the desert floor, their weapons locked and loaded, their crews in full battle dress.

There were six of them, moving very quickly, line abreast, leaving a mighty cloud of smoke and dust behind. In that dirty wake, nearly obscured, was a second column, this one made up of a dozen Strykers, the U.S. military's highly advanced, heavily armed personnel carrier. Each Stryker carried either a 105mm cannon, a couple 40mm grenade launchers, or a trio of 50-caliber machine guns, this in addition to eight fully armed soldiers within, plus a three-man crew. Aligned in three units of four each, the Stryker drivers were propelling their futuristic APCs ahead at full throttle, trying their best to keep up with the speeding M1 tanks—and not get lost in the dust cloud while doing it.

Behind the Strykers were six Humvees; they too were traveling at high speed, their drivers pedal to the metal in an effort to keep up with the speeding armored column. These superjeeps were armed with all kinds of weapons, from 50-caliber machine guns, to top-mounted TOW missile launches, to grenade-launching automatic cannons.

Normally, the Humvees would be leading this sort of maneuver, followed by the Strykers and then the M1s. But this was not anything normal happening here. This was an all-out race to get to a point about ten miles farther out in the desert. If the column's intelligence was right, an enemy was waiting there, completely unaware, just begging to be destroyed.

This collection of war-fighting machines was code-named Zulu Force One. The enemy had been designated "Al-Saheed Bedun." Roughly translated: ghosts of the sand. The Zulus had been out here in the desert for the past week, trying to track them down. But these ghosts proved a slippery lot. They were an airborne unit, with a dozen helicopters—gunships and troop carriers—and more than four dozen soldiers. Zulu Force One didn't know much more about them than that, other than the fact that destroying them, right now, was paramount to all things Zulu. Thus, the headlong rush across the desert.

It was 0530 hours. Though the sun was beginning to paint the eastern desert peaks in a warm orange hue, daylight was still about twenty minutes away. No matter what time of day, though, any chance to catch the elusive enemy copters on the ground had to be exploited

The report said as many as eight of the dozen enemy opters might be stuck on the ground.

THE HEADLONG DASH ACROSS THE DESERT FINALLY reached a mountain pass named Apache Ridge. It was a mile long road that led out of this valley and into the next. According to Zulu intelligence, the enemy was grounded somewhere on the other side.

The armored column came to a halt halfway up Apache. Having been forced to revert to a more typical military line, the Humvees now raced to the front. Two were equipped with long-range NightScope cameras, still highly effective even with the coming of dawn. They would be able to see things over in the next valley that the rest of Zulu could not.

These two vehicles crested the ridge while the column waited anxiously in the pass below. It took just five minutes to videoscan the entire valley, then the Humvees hurriedly returned to the command Stryker, bearing their results. Inserting the surveillance disk into the Stryker's main control console, the column's officers saw both good news and bad news.

There were indeed helicopters on the ground in the next valley over. Four of them could be clearly seen about a mile away through the emerald glaze of the video camera's NightScope telephoto lens. And shadowy figures could be seen shuttling around these four

by Zulu Force One—even if it meant routine
procedures, such as discouraging moving line al
had to be dispensed with. That's how bad Zulu
wanted these guys.

It was easy to understand why. The helicopters
been making fools of Zulu for the past seven d
They'd fought ten skirmishes in that time—and
Zulus had gotten the worst of it every time. More d
heartening, the copters had twice surprised the armore
force while it was refueling, the most vulnerable posi
tion for a mechanized column to be in during combat.
The ghostly copters had put the hurt on Zulu Force One
both these times too. So again, the revenge motive was
red-lining high for the armored force.

Not two hours before, the Zulus had been handed a
gift. Just as the copters' twin attacks on the armored
column during its refueling cycle had undoubtedly
been due to some valuable bit of intelligence the enemy
had secured, Zulu had come to possess an incredible piece of information. By way of an anonymous
asset—a satellite perhaps, or even some guy sitting
at a gaming computer—Zulu Force One had learned
the enemy copter force was presently grounded in an
exposed part of the desert, due to heavy winds and
rainstorms that had swept through the area even earlier that morning. Moreover, there was a good chance
some of the copters were having mechanical problems—chopper engines did not like the desert or the
dust that came with it.

copters, as if they were trying to fix them. So that much of the intelligence gem had been correct.

But, strangely, this didn't seem to be the right valley. As depicted on the satellite maps that accompanied Zulu's newfound intelligence, the valley where the enemy was supposedly located was flat, wide-open and free of any obstructions, save the odd gulley here and there. Yet the NightScope images clearly showed small islands of tug brush and bramble scattered around the disabled copters, indeed throughout the whole valley. Some of the vegetation appeared fifteen feet tall in some places, while less in others.

The Zulu commanders deigned the unexpected vegetation an aberration, then didn't give it a second thought. The enemy copters were down there, and Zulu wanted to take them out for good. They sent word to the rest of the column: We're going in.

The column proceeded over Apache Ridge and into the next valley. Once back on the desert floor, the advance toward the enemy would begin in earnest. But this time the Zulu commanders arrayed their assets in a more military fashion. The column realigned itself into three combat teams, each consisting of two tanks, four Strykers, and two Humvees. This was mobile all-terrain firepower, concentrated in its most deadly fashion. For Zulu Force One, it was can't-miss.

One last order was given and the column started out again. Engines growling, the three combat teams screeched their way into the night, charging right at the gaggle of copters not a mile away. The slightly rolling terrain, lingering darkness, and pure surprise would all work to their advantage. Each team put its Strykers out front, to utilize one of the twenty-first century APC's best attributes: Unlike the old-style APCs, or tanks or Humvees, Strykers made almost no noise when they moved. Sitting atop eight huge rubber tires, instead of tracks, the heavily armed vehicles were nearly silent by design. Whether in the hills of Afghanistan or a crowded village in Iraq, any enemy caught dozing by the muted approach almost always paid with his life.

Zulu's battle plan was simple. Once the Strykers hit, the Humvees, traveling right behind, would angle their way into the enemy's rear, surrounding them. At that point the M1 tanks would arrive and the grounded copters would be toast.

And this is how it began. The three teams barreled toward the enemy position, streaking by the islands of sage bush and crooked tug trees that had somehow missed being photographed by their intelligence assets. A dust storm began kicking up ahead of them, another advantage for the Zulus. The more sand and dust swirling around, the less likely that any of the enemy copters still able to fly would be nearby. Zulu would come right out of the wind, literally falling upon the enemy before he knew what hit him. Attack in strength and surprise—and give no quarter. This was what units like Zulu Force One did best.

*   *   *

AS IT TURNED OUT, THE CREW OF THE LAST HUMVEE in the third combat team unintentionally stalled their vehicle just as the charge began. It was a momentary problem—the driver quickly restarted the engine and they were soon off as well. But the slight delay meant this Humvee was left trailing the rest of the attack force. That's how its crew got to see one of the most incredible scenes ever witnessed on a modern field of battle.

The rest of Zulu Force One was about 1,000 feet out ahead of the trailing Humvee; the Hummer's two front-seat crewmen, as well as the weapons operator in the top turret, had the entire field of battle stretched out before them. They were wearing their NightScope goggles, the wind and blowing dust adding to the surre-alistic wash of green flashing before their eyes. Though they were trying to speed up, they were still behind the main force when they passed the largest cluster of desert vegetation.

That's when it got weird. No sooner had the cloud of dust trailing the main force settled down when the large clumps of vegetation started to move. This was not due to the wind—the flora wasn't blowing side to side. In-stead, it was moving upward, and doing so very fast. As incredible as it seemed, the miniforest of bramble was shooting straight up in the air.

In the next few seconds this strange image began to make some sense. The vegetation was being torn away as it ascended. Revealed beneath it were helicopters. Black helicopters—heavily armed, almost silent, eight of them.

The Sand Ghosts.

They had appeared again.

The Humvee crew was astonished. The people flying the copters had hidden them so well, they'd blended right into the landscape, to be totally disregarded by the attacking force. This wasn't just camouflage used to its extreme. This was something else, something almost otherworldly.

The Humvee crew watched as the helicopters, all shapes and sizes, leveled off at twenty-five feet and started moving forward, chasing the rest of Zulu even as Zulu was charging toward the handful of disabled copters. But then another surprise: Those disabled aircraft were disabled no more. They too were rising into the green night—not broken down, just pretending to be that way. As one, these four copters turned toward the tip of Zulu's vanguard, while the trailing copters fell into slightly curved flight paths behind. The crew of the trailing Humvee knew exactly what was happening: The copters were performing a classic envelopment maneuver—in the dark, in a dust storm, only twenty-five feet above the ground.

The driver of the trailing Humvee let out a stream of obscenities.

"*Who the fuck are these guys?*" he cried.

Zulu Force Once had been fooled again . . .

Just as all this was happening, the sun finally topped the peaks to the east. In seconds the darkened valley was bathed in brilliant early morning sunlight. Just like that, there was no longer any need to use NightVision goggles. Everyone in Zulu could see what was unfolding right before their eyes.

Not unlike real Apaches surrounding a troop of blundering 7th Cavalry, the helicopters quickly had Zulu surrounded. In just those few seconds, the armored force realized it was doomed. The copters had played them perfectly—again. *That* was the maddening thing.

Though losing steam, the armored column finally reached its destination. The small flat circle of ground where the "disabled" copters had been parked was empty now—not even a grease spot or a puddle of aviation oil left behind as proof that anything had been there at all.

This unexpected turn of events, this elaborate ruse by the copter men who somehow made desert trees fly, caused understandable confusion among Zulu Force One. Some of the Strykers rolled right through the target area. Behind them the M1s and the Humvees began to scatter too, their one concern now was how the hell to break out of the aerial encirclement.

But it proved impossible. Not only were the copters brimming with electronic interference equipment, scrambling just about every electrical device found aboard the tanks, the high-tech APCs, and the Humvees—they were also filled with armed troops, many of them aiming their weapons at the armored vehicles. The copters were banking even closer to the stalled attack force, corralling those trying to break out of the fatal squeeze, making the noose around Zulu even tighter.

It didn't take long—maybe twenty seconds at most. But finally every vehicle in Zulu ground to a halt. The situation was hopeless and they knew it. The armored column remained still and awaited its fate. Smelling blood, the copters began circling even tighter around the trapped vehicles. The doomed men on the ground were all thinking the same thing: Just get it over with. Do it right, but do it quick.

And the copters began to do just that, when . . . suddenly . . . the din was broken by another sound.

A car horn, blaring.

Everything stopped. Deep in the blowing sand, a pair of headlights could be seen, piercing the dust-driven storm. The honking horn became more insistent and closer. An instant later a huge black Chevy SUV burst into view. It roared past the trapped armored column, screeching to a halt in front of the command Stryker.

A mid-sized man in a natty Army dress uniform emerged from the passenger seat and began waving his arms, this while the SUV's horn continued its high-pitched bleating. Everyone got the message. The armored column turned off its weapons' systems and lowered its guns. The helicopters broke out of their encircling maneuver and began landing among Zulu's armored vehicles. Suddenly the desert floor was very crowded.

Soldiers began jumping out of tanks and Strykers, just as crew members deplaned from their helicopters. Some bad feelings boiled over, and there were a few shoving matches, but nothing serious. The soldiers gathered around the SUV as the well dressed Army major climbed atop its hood so he could be seen by everybody. Finally the SUV's driver stopped honking his horn.

"OK, gather around," the Army officer told the dusty soldiers. "Can everyone hear me?"

A grumbled reply. Yes, he could be heard.

"OK—we have to end this drill right now," he began. "Prematurely, but immediately."

There was a groan from the crowd, coming almost entirely from the helicopter force. They'd been on the brink of a stunning victory. To have it snatched away from them by the little man atop the SUV was a huge disappointment. Their whole reason for being out here was to beat the Zulu mud huggers. But now, for all their efforts, they were getting . . . a speech.

"This one will go into the books as a draw, a push," the officer told them. More grumbling. "Something has come up in Washington which makes all this necessary."

He turned to the commander of Zulu Force One. "Your new orders are to return to your barracks back at Fort Irwin, and stand down. Someone from Training Command will be in touch."

That's all the ground force guys needed to hear. For this exercise, their name had been Zulu Force One. But they were better known as OpFor, as in Opposition

Force. This desert, part of the U.S. military's National Training Center, was their playground, their permanent assignment. Other units came out here to learn how to fight in the desert; OpFor provided the in-house, on-site enemy. Their weapons real, but not deadly. Their ammunition, laser beams that made you "dead" without killing you. It was all about war gaming, and just by experience alone, OpFor was supposed to be the best in the world at it.

Until the Sand Ghosts came along.

FOR MOST UNITS ASSIGNED TO FIGHT IN THE VAST war gaming site, the NTC was a hell on earth. To its north was no less than Death Valley. To the east, the Mojave Desert. To the west, the China Lake Naval Weapons Center, a place where all kinds of ordnance, some of it top secret, was exploded on a daily basis. No matter how highly trained or talented, visiting teams rarely did good here.

Yet the nasty two-week engagement against the helicopter force had been the hardest fought exercise in OpFor's history. And the copters had kicked ass at every turn, in OpFor's own backyard. Not a pleasant outcome for the resident desert soldiers.

None of this would make the seventy-five-mile trip back to their barracks any easier. Still, OpFor departed without much fanfare, forming up in a typical line column and rumbling away into the growing sunlight.

All that remained now was the copter force. They drew even tighter around the Army officer. They knew him: Major Jim Shaw, DIA, NRO, NSA, and attached to a very top secret Pentagon think tank, known as the Special Projects Division.

And he was one of the few people in the U.S. military who knew *them*: Task Force 160, U.S. Army Aviation, Special Attached Aerial Battalion. Their official unit name was the "Sky Hunters." But they were better known as X-Battalion.

They were the blackest special operations unit in the U.S. military. Where the 160th's regular air battalions served as high-tech taxis, moving Rangers, or SEALs or Delta Force, in and out of harm's way, the X-Battalion was a small Special Forces' army unto itself. Each member was specialized not only in his duty pertaining to one of their twelve helicopters—pilots, crew chiefs, gunners—but was also a skilled Special Forces warfighter on the ground. In fact, they were more highly trained than those more famous secret warriors that the rest of TF-160 spent their time flying around.

After being formed, ironically, by a misguided conception from the Pentagon a year before, XBat first proved its mettle under some extremely harsh basic training, and then in the North Korean mountains where it was sent to look for a wayward nuclear device that had the ability to snuff out all life on Planet Earth. Many U.S. Special Forces units had been sent into North Korea to search for this Doomsday Bomb. But it was XBat who not only found it, but had to battle an entire North Korean division in order snatch the bomb away and, literally, save the world.

This was how the unit made its bones. They'd been unorthodox in their methods, but their success had raised their profile in the eyes of key military people in Washington. The unit was given new helicopters to replace the ones lost during the action in North Korea. They were also given new uniforms, black camos with a unit patch showing the constellation Orion—the original Sky Hunter—with a large red X going through it. They looked cool and they acted cool.

Their second mission was no less exciting. XBat had flown deep into the South American jungle to stomp one of the world's most notorious cocaine dealers, a man who'd planned to flood the U.S. with a particularly potent strain of "supercrack." They left no one standing at this ultracriminal's processing plant, nor at his multi-million-dollar jungle mansion. In less than ten minutes XBat scored as big a victory in the war on drugs as decades of work by every other U.S. antidrug agency combined.

What followed, though, was a mission within a mission—and this one had XBat going back into the upper Amazon jungle, where, against all odds, they found an ICBM site under construction by the Venezuelan military. This base's missiles were armed, fueled, and ready for launch . . . against the United States. The situation quickly went from bad to worse, as shortly before XBat discovered the missile base, the Venezuelans had discovered XBat. Realizing the copter force had been hiding inside their country and running operations against its brutally repressive military, Venezuela declared war on the United States—technically, anyway. The declaration was made through the lowest possible diplomatic channel, and only a handful of people in Washington even knew it was sent. Still, the warheads atop the Venezuelan ICBMs were all too real, and hotheads inside the Venezuelan government had given the order for them to launch. If it hadn't been for XBat destroying the ICBMs when they did, the southern edge of the United States would have been turned into a nuclear wasteland—surely causing the U.S. to retaliate in kind and wipe Venezuela off the map.

So, twice XBat had saved the U.S. and the world from catastrophe. They were heroes, *real* heroes. A brutally efficient force, brimming with self-confidence, proven to have beaten the best.

Which would make what Shaw had to tell them even more difficult.

"I am here on orders from the National Security Council and signed off by the President," he began. "I've been asked to inform you that your mission has been completed. You proved that an element of TF-160 could be mobile and self-sufficient. That was your duty statement a little over a year ago. You've passed with flying colors."

The unit members let out a hearty if surprised cheer.

It was nice to finally be noticed by the civilian higher-ups for saving the world, not once but twice.

Shaw let a respectable amount of silence go by. Then he added: "And that's why, as of this moment, they are disbanding this unit and wiping it off the books."

A gasp echoed across the empty desert. *Disbanding the unit? We're the best unit on the planet . . .*

Troopers began shouting angry questions up at Shaw. But the well-groomed Army officer had come prepared. He held the yellow envelope containing their orders over his head and barked: "Any questions, put them in writing to your CO. That's all, gentlemen. Dismissed."

With that, Shaw came down off the hood and tried to climb back into the SUV. He was madly signaling his driver to start the engine for a fast getaway.

But a very strong hand caught Shaw's elbow before he could close his door. Shaw turned to face his assailant—it was XBat's CO, Colonel Bobby Autry.

Autry was not one to tangle with. He was in his fifties, fit, rock-jawed, movie star rugged. He was also a very determined individual who would break Shaw in two if necessary to get what he needed.

And what he needed right now was an explanation.

Shaw did his best to thrust the yellow orders envelope into Autry's other hand and say his goodbye, but Autry made sure he wasn't going anywhere. He calmly but firmly pulled Shaw from the SUV and escorted him through the crowd of troopers, stopping only once they'd reached a deserted spot next to one of the unit's souped-up copters, out of earshot of the others.

It was clear Autry was furious. Even after he let Shaw go, he had to take a moment to regain his composure.

Finally, he spoke: "Please tell me the *real* reason this is happening. And spare me the 'Mission Accomplished' bullshit, Jim. We've been through a lot over the years. You owe me that at least."

Shaw couldn't argue. They'd known each other since the 1980s. What's more, Shaw had been there at the creation of XBat. And in the times XBat found itself in trouble, he had helped them over the rough patches. All XBat had done in return was save the world, twice.

Now he was here to deliver their death notice—and Autry was smart enough to know there was another reason, beyond the official explanation.

Shaw took a deep breath. He didn't like this any more than Autry. But he owed the senior officer the truth.

"The background thinking is this," he began. "You almost caused World War Three with Venezuela. I mean, you guys caused an *actual* war—two days long and very secret. But it still happened. And you also went so far off the map in North Korea that you've caught the attention of the New Thinkers in the administration. And believe me, they really didn't take a liking to you."

Autry was still angry, not surprised. He began kicking the dust at his feet.

Shaw went on: "And there's another thing, Bobby.

You're embarrassing all the other units out there. I mean, Special Forces are now the darlings of DC, and it just doesn't look good when they are spending billions of dollars on those guys, and *you* guys keep beating them at their own games—and doing it on a shoestring."

He looked out on the vast training center desert; the last of the dust cloud being churned up by the retreating OpFor column was just fading from view. "Just like you just embarrassed those guys. Just like you leapfrogged over all those special ops teams in North Korea. And taking on the entire country of Venezuela? By yourselves? That kind of stuff makes its way around in the special ops world very quickly, no matter how secret you are. And frankly, it's seen as bad for morale."

Autry shook his head. "So, we're *too* good, *too* cheap, and we made the mistake of preventing not one, but two nuclear wars. That's why they're ending the mission?"

Shaw nodded. "It's crazy, I know."

Autry looked back toward his men. The news was finally beginning to sink in. He thought a moment.

"Well," he finally drawled, "at least my guys will all go on to bigger and better things."

But Shaw was shaking his head again. "You didn't hear me right on one thing, Bobby," he said. "I didn't say they were just ending the mission. I said they were *disbanding* the unit. Wiping it right off the books. *No one* is going on to other units. They're dispersing you to the four winds. I thought it was wise to leave it to you to explain that part to your men. They don't want to hear a death sentence coming from a cog like me."

Now, Autry could barely speak. "But that's absolutely nuts," he protested. "Look at the valuable experience this country will be losing. The way those guys fight? The way they fly those helicopters? The way they *hide* those helicopters? They're going to let all that just go away?"

Shaw shrugged. "Yes, they are," he said solemnly. "And the reason is that they don't want anyone knowing about you—no one who doesn't already, that is. Like I said, this was a top secret mission, but you also managed to put some of the high and mighty thinkers in their places, and that doesn't go over well anywhere inside the Beltway. If you guys were spread throughout the special ops community, your story will travel on and on forever. But if they cut you down now—everything will die away in a few months, the stories, the whispers. In a year, people will wonder if you ever existed. In five years, you'll be forgotten."

The two men were silent for a long time. Then Shaw patted Autry on the shoulder. "That's the way they want it," he told the XBat commander. "And though it breaks my heart to say this, Bobby, that's the way it's got to be."

Autry stood frozen for a long time. His head was spinning. But finally he turned back to Shaw. "OK,

Jimmy," he said, shaking the officer's hand. "I know it was tough for you to come out here to tell me this. Thanks for being straight with me."

They slowly walked back to the SUV. The rest of XBat had dispersed by then.

Shaw climbed inside the SUV. "My advice?" he said to Autry. "Just stay as low-key and as healthy as possible. You'll get your official muster-out orders in two days. You've got food, you've got shelter. And those copters are air-conditioned, right? Just stay out here, in place, until the orders get to you. No one will bother you until then, I promise. The break will give you and your guys a chance to let this all sink in."

He lowered his voice a bit, then went on: "Now, officially, they've asked me to keep an eye on you. But you guys don't need a babysitter. Just don't take any risks; I wouldn't even fly if you don't have to. There's no sense in getting yourself or one of your guys killed now—for nothing."

With that, Shaw gave his driver the signal and the SUV drove away.

TEN MINUTES LATER BOBBY AUTRY WAS STANDING on the peak of a nearby mountain.

He'd flown up here, alone, in one of the unit's AH-6 "Flying Eggs." He'd started out in TF-160 flying the small buglike copter. And now, today, he knew this might be the last time he'd be able to fly one again.

There weren't too many copters like the AH-6 where he was going.

He still couldn't believe it—the Army was putting him out to pasture. He was still numb from head to toe, cold in his bones, his heart no longer beating in his chest. The end of XBat meant the end of his career, it was as simple as that. He'd been on the verge of forced retirement when the XBat mission came along; taking it had prolonged his time in service by another year. He should be happy with that, he tried to tell himself now. But it still hurt.

So this was how it ended . . . Shoved aside? Lost in the shuffle? Dealing with people who didn't even know your name? Autry spit off the side of the cliff. This wasn't just his job. It was *his life*. He'd spent nearly a quarter century in TF-160 before XBat came along. He'd been involved in many of the Nightstalkers' major operations over the years. Lebanon. Rwanda. Cuba. Moscow. His specialty was going in and getting people out of tough situations, and some of the stuff he'd done was so classified even the other members of the TF-160 didn't know about it. Bottom line: He'd given his all to Army Aviation. To his country. To his men. He'd been shot down twice. Wounded more times than he could count. He'd lost half his hearing. He'd lost his hair. He'd lost his wife.

And for what? To be kicked out, simply for doing his job *too* well?

Thank you, Uncle Sam . . .

And his troops . . . They too had given their every-thing. *Especially* the guys in XBat. He'd worked with some great soldiers throughout his career, but it was his present command that held the most extraordinary. Considered borderline and unfit to serve in the regular TF-160 battalions, they'd been dumped into XBat as little more than a broad hint that they should just quit the Army before they were pushed. What they did instead was shoot their way to the top, until even the dopes in Washington recognized that they were the best. And now they were history . . . just like him.

Or not even history. They were being wiped right off the map. Like Shaw said, in no time at all no one would even know XBat ever existed. Like dying without a gravestone. It was no way to go.

Not more than a year before, at the birth of XBat, Autry had given a speech that changed his life. The new unit had taken up quarters in a pre–World War Two air-field deep in the bug-infested swamps of Georgia. Autry had just been assigned the impossible task of forming the experimental unit—but at the time, he wanted no part of it. Just minutes before addressing his men for the first time he'd learned that he would be able to get a quick ticket out of the swamp, and out of the fledgling unit completely. All he had to do was leave the rest of his men behind.

He just couldn't do it, though—and no one was more surprised than himself. That night, up on the makeshift stage in the unit's mess hall, looking out at the faces,

he'd had a religious experience. Instead of using his pull
to get reassigned to a cushy desk job, he laid out a plan
with which the unit could not only train itself the way
the deep thinkers in Washington wanted them to, but
also to deliver a major Fuck You to those same deep
thinkers who in a million years never thought it could
be done. That night bonded XBat for life. That night
allowed them to go off and do great things.

And their reputation since? Shaw was right—it
was off the charts. They weren't just the superstars of
America's Special Forces these days. Their name was
being whispered around the globe, in the backrooms,
in the bazaars, in the vast underworld of international
troublemakers where criminals, dictators and terrorists
would think twice before stirring up trouble, just on the
possibility that XBat might come to get *them* too.

But now those days were gone.

The trouble was in Autry's perceptions—and he knew
it. XBat became so good, so fast, he'd simply assumed
it would never end. That they'd go on forever. That this
day would never come. But now it was here. So suddenly . . .

The kick in the stomach.

The knife in the back.

His heart, worn-out.

Not ticking.

Just dead . . .

He shielded his eyes and looked out on the vast
desert. It was still only 0700 hours—seven in the

morning—but already this was one of the worst days of his life. To the east, the sun was rising in the most glorious way. The sky was awash in reds and yellow and pink, bathing him in bare warmth. The air smelled clean. From one end of the horizon to the other, the sky was crystal clear.

To the west, though, it was a different story. Out over the Pacific were the worst storm clouds he'd ever seen. Gigantic, black and roiling, Autry felt a chill run through him just looking at them. The clouds were a sign from above—and not a pleasant one. *That's* what awaited him now. The stormy murk, nothing but turbulence and darkness, lay ahead. He knew no other life but the military. He didn't know *how* to be a civilian. And that scared him the most.

He collapsed onto nearby rock. Strangely, at that moment, with his life seemingly draining out of him, thoughts of his wife began flooding in. If this had all been a waste, if he'd sacrificed himself for so many years for the Army only to get cut off at the knees, then the greatest crime of all was losing his wife.

He'd loved her from the moment he'd set eyes on her, this high school sweetheart who turned into a beautiful woman right before his eyes. The problem was, he also loved his country, and every time the choice came down between the two of them, he'd picked the job. They'd had eight really good years of marriage and a few more not so great. Most of all, she hated the constant moving around. And that's why she left him finally, settling somewhere in northern California after thirteen years together. Since then he'd screwed up at least a dozen chances at a possible reconciliation, again, because he thought duty to the Army came first. Looking back on it now, though, he realized how foolish a choice that had been.

And *that's* why he was feeling so low now. Looking out, literally from the mountaintop—yes, that was his future off to the west. Nothing but storm clouds and heavy winds.

Certainly not weather to fly into alone.

HE GOT UP EVENTUALLY AND STARTED TO CLIMB BACK into the AH-6. One boot in, though, he heard an unusual noise behind him. High-pitched, yet distorted by the early morning air.

Strange . . .

He turned to see a small black helicopter approaching swiftly from the east.

It roared right by him, then began a quick descent into the valley where the rest of XBat had set up their temporary bivouac.

Autry recognized the helicopter right away, that was the weird thing. He'd seen it many times. All-black Textron. Unmarked. Tinted canopy glass.

The copter belonged to the CIA, XBat's frequent partner in crime.

What the hell do they want? he thought.

*   *   *

WHEN HE ARRIVED BACK AT THE BIVOUAC, AUTRY
found the all-black helicopter sitting next to XBat's CH-
47 Chinook command craft.

Three people were sitting up on the Chinook's flight
deck. Two were his XOs, Captains Mungo and Mc-
Cune. Both were great pilots, great officers and great
soldiers. As individuals, though, they were as different
as night and day.

At twenty-three, McCune was the youngest officer
in the unit. That he harbored a secret desire to fly jet
fighters was no surprise—he flew his helicopter like it
was an F-16 stuck in afterburner. Originally assigned to
TF-160's operations in Iraq, McCune had been relieved
of combat duty for committing "overly aggressive ac-
tions during sensitive military operations." Translation:
He was nuts. That aggressiveness proved a godsend for
XBat, though, as it was McCune who'd saved the unit
from annihilation during the North Korean operation.
A native of the tough Boston streets, the pug-nosed but
handsome pilot was boisterous and verbose. He was a
favorite among the men.

Mungo, on the other hand, was not. He'd never been
accused of being anyone's favorite, in or out of XBat.
Years before, when he too was part of the regular TF-
160, he was supposed to fly the infamous Black Hawk
Down mission into Mogadishu, Somalia. However,
after claiming a vague illness—and displaying a pair of

slit wrists—he missed the operation and as a result had been forever labeled a coward within the Nightstalker community. Mungo had always been close-lipped about what really happened to him that day, why he had chickened out just when TF-160 needed him most. He'd actually sued the Army later on to keep him in special ops, but upon winning the case was relegated to shit duty—that is, until, like McCune, he was plucked from obscurity and put in XBat. The irony was, this quiet, moody Texan had also done some incredibly heroic things during the murderous North Korean operation, and during XBat's recent harrowing adventure in Venezuela as well.

The third man sitting in the copter was Gary Weir. He was a senior CIA field officer—and within his office in Washington, DC, he was known as the busiest man in the Agency. The all-black, tricked-out Textron copter belonged to him.

Like Autry, Weir was in his early fifties, though he looked much younger. He had a head full of Kennedyesque hair and a mind like a supercomputer. He and Autry first met during the invasion of Grenada in 1983. Autry's first combat assignment for TF-160 was to fly Weir—then a lowly CIA photo analyst pressed into duty—over a very high priority target hanging off the edge of the tiny embattled Caribbean island. (They were promptly shot down.) Their paths crossed again at the beginning of the North Korean adventure, and Weir had been intertwined with XBat ever since.

As usual, Weir was gulping down coffee when Autry climbed in. The CIA man was in the middle of briefing the two junior XBat officers and didn't slow down a bit at Autry's arrival. Just a quick handshake and a mock salute.

"Colonel, as I was telling your guys here, we've got a rather sticky situation you should be aware of."

Autry laughed at him. "A mission, you mean?"

Weir nodded. "Yes—something that has to be done, like right now. Today. *This morning*. That's why I'm so glad I found you people out here. You're just the guys for the job."

Autry looked at Mungo and McCune. They just shrugged.

"You haven't told him yet?" Autry asked them.

Both shook their heads. Weir was excitable, in that intellectual sort of way. Once he got going, it was sometimes hard to slow him down.

But Autry knew there was no sense keeping *this* from him. He held up the yellow envelope containing XBat's last orders.

"We can't do your mission," he told Weir.

The CIA agent stopped slurping his coffee. "What do you mean? Why not?"

"Because we're no longer a functioning unit," Autry replied soberly. "They just closed us down."

Weir stared back at him like he had two heads. He took the orders from Autry's hand, opened the envelope and quickly read the two pages within. "They're giving *you guys* the boot?" he gasped, astonished. "Are they crazy?"

Autry just shrugged.

"But you're the best special op team ever," Weir insisted.

Autry shrugged again. "Apparently that was the problem."

Weir re-read the orders, then furrowed his brow in deep thought—for about two seconds. Then he simply tore the orders in two.

The copter pilots were stunned.

"My apologies to Major Shaw," Weir declared. "But this is too important for those morons in Washington to fuck up. Consider those orders moot. You're doing this mission . . . case closed."

With that, Weir lit a cigarette and pulled open his laptop.

On the screen was an image of the Coast Guard cutter *Steadfast*.

WEIR HAD A STRANGE STORY TO TELL.

"Not forty-eight hours ago," he began, "this Coast Guard vessel was attempting to assist the crews of two cargo ships about seventy-five miles off Los Angeles. Due to this freaky storm, the Coast Guard guys had been pulling people out of the water for nearly a week. They came upon these two tramps, sailing in the middle of the storm but off the normal shipping lanes. The freighters were apparently traveling together, and when the cutter arrived on the scene, they thought one or both were sinking."

He switched to another image on the laptop. This one was a long-range, computer-enhanced video clip taken from space by Galaxy Net, the top-secret, highly intelligent, but supremely troublesome spy satellite network run by the NSA for use only by America's most elite special ops units. The slight yellowish tint to the video was the giveaway. Marked "Image Cluster Number 1," it showed three ships being tossed about in extremely stormy seas. One of the vessels was identified as the *Steadfast*. The other two were obviously cargo ships. Rusty and beat-up, one had a bright red stack, the other's stack was dull yellow.

"The *Steadfast*'s land base was in contact with them during this entire incident," Weir went on. "As you can see in this image, the cutter got pretty close to the two cargo ships, again thinking they were in trouble. Now watch this . . ."

As the words were leaving his mouth, a huge wave was seen coming out of the top of the frame. It hit the three ships simultaneously, rolling them over like toys in a bathtub. When the image cleared, all that remained was the empty, storm-tossed ocean.

"Son of a bitch," Autry exclaimed. "That thing must have been a hundred feet high. Those ships never had a chance—not with that wave."

Weir laughed darkly. "If it *was* a wave," he said.

The three copter pilots were mystified. "What do you mean?" Autry asked him.

Weir cued another video clip. Marked "Image Cluster Number 2," it began exactly as the first, showing the three ships, very close to each other, with the storm raging around them.

"So?" Autry asked.

"Just watch," Weir told him.

They counted down the seconds until disaster struck—but this time, instead of a devastating wave suddenly washing over the ships, a huge explosion went off. Blinding, it lit up the stormy night for miles.

McCune exclaimed: "Jesus, what the hell was that? A nuclear bomb?"

Weir shook his head. "We don't know," he said. "But it was some powerful blast, whatever it was."

The video clip showed a cloud of smoke lingering over the area for a few moments before being blown away. The two cargo ships could barely be seen, rocking mightily in the explosion's wake. That's where the tape ended.

Two video recordings of the same incident, but each with a different outcome? It seemed crazy. But for people familiar with the Galaxy Net, it was no great surprise.

"So, it's 'drunk' again?" Autry asked Weir dryly.

Weir nodded. "Like it's been mainlining Grey Goose."

The XBat pilots knew all about the problems with the

Galaxy Net. When it was working right, the ultraso-phisticated surveillance system could show any point on Earth, close-up, clearly and in three-D, in both real-time video *and* audio—a fantastic tool for U.S. intelligence services. But that wasn't all. Through its massive arrays of microcircuitry, the Galaxy Net was also designed to look for and identify any potential security threats to the United States. In this mode, if it spotted something suspicious, it would not only record the event, but, by engaging its huge capacity for artificial intelligence, it could visually *push* the event ahead a few moments in time, like a computer game, showing the observer what *might* happen next in any particular situation, and giv-ing a major heads-up on what could be done about it.

For instance, if the Galaxy Net was being used to spy on a battlefield in the Middle East, its cameras might detect a tank column coming from one direction, and troops equipped with antitank weapons coming from the other. The G-Net would be able to process this in-formation, weigh all the factors, even count the number of weapons on each side, and then play out the most likely scenario of how the pending battle might turn out—all in a matter of nanoseconds. If there were more tanks than antitank weapons, the G-Net would actually show, in lifelike graphics, the tanks winning the day. In other words, the Galaxy Net was designed to look into the future.

But there was a problem. The orbital spy system was so complex—or as some claimed, never built correctly—it sometimes mixed up the reality portion of its artificial brain with its five-minutes-from-now side, literally making it difficult to distinguish between reality and virtuality. Sometimes, as presented by the Galaxy Net, both appeared to be one and the same.

This was not a minor concern. Consisting of dozens of satellites, the Galaxy Net cost hundreds of billions of dollars to launch and operate—and still much of its potential, to do many things, lay untapped. Yet it was also full of glitches. In situations like this, when its universe of sensors were obviously not working correctly, the question was always: Should we believe it or not? In many ways, it *was* like staring into a trillion-dollar crystal ball that somehow had a drinking problem.

"This is the communications tape we got from the cutter's home port," Weir went on, pushing another button on his laptop. "They were monitoring the bridge's radio traffic at the time of the incident."

He let the audio portion run. Right away, voices could be heard crying out in the confusion and noise. The tape picked up at least two people talking anxiously. One was clearly heard to say: *"Jesus—what the hell is that?"*

Then the tape ran out.

"That's scary, man," McCune said. "Very creepy."

"So did the CG vessel blow up?" Autry asked wearily. "Or did it go down after being hit by one mutha of a wave?"

He'd directed the question to Weir, but the CIA agent

remained mute. He lit another cigarette. Autry sensed Weir knew more than he was letting on.

"You have something else to add, my friend?" he asked the spy.

Weir shifted nervously in his seat, obviously fighting some demons within.

"OK, I give up," he said, almost mumbling. "There is one more element to this. But it's so top secret that if I tell you, not only will I have to kill you, I'll have to kill myself too . . ."

The XBat pilots groaned. How many times had they heard *that* joke?

"Just spill it," Autry told him. "We're all grown-ups here."

Weir took a deep breath. "OK—here it is, short and sweet: There's a chance the Galaxy Net itself sank that cutter—by mistake."

The pilots were stunned. "The *G-Net* did it?" McCune said. "How the hell . . ."

Autry was floored. "You mean that thing is a weapon too?"

Weir just looked at his burning cigarette. "It's a lot of things," he said under his breath. "It's crammed full of stuff they sent up when the satellites were first launched, stuff they could further develop here on the ground at a later date. It's constantly being updated, and personally, that's what I think keeps screwing it up. But, that said, one element of its untapped abilities—perhaps—is being able to concentrate enough electronic interference on a certain point that everything connected to a computer just goes *blewy!* A large chain reaction results and things start blowing up. Big things, little things. Things with thick skins. A missile site. A weapons' factory. A command bunker—"

"A ship?" Autry interrupted him.

Weir nodded slowly. "Yeah, maybe—but again, a total fuck-up. A total mistake."

McCune was astonished. "You mean killer satellites are flying around up there? Hitting the wrong stuff?"

Weir could only repeat himself. "Yeah—maybe."

The young pilot leaned back in his seat. "Now that's *very* fucked up," he said, a master of the understatement. "That thing is nothing but a trillion-dollar piece of junk. Why don't they just scrap it? Shut it down?"

Weir laughed darkly. "Do you want to be the guy who goes into the Oval Office and breaks that kind of news? That a trillion dollars just went up in smoke?"

Weir lit another cigarette. "Besides, it *does* work, when it's doing the routine surveillance, eavesdropping and illegal spying stuff. And just by that alone, the military is addicted to it. And so is the Agency, the NSA, you name it—anyone who can plug his modem into it. But when it fucks up—it fucks up *big*-time."

Weir took a long drag of his cigarette. He looked nervous. Not like him.

"Either way," he went on, "explosion or tidal wave, that Coast Guard cutter is gone. The CG has been out there looking for it for two days and nights. But they haven't found so as much as an oil slick."

Another stream of smoke blew across the flight deck.

"Now, all this couldn't have happened at a worse time," Weir said. "And that's where you guys come in. The southern California area is going to be extremely busy in the next two days—securitywise, that is. Every spare intelligence op has been flown into Los Angeles, even some secretaries and bookkeepers. Shit, half the Agency is out here. And it's not just us. All our cousins are out here too: NSA, DIA, FBI, Homeland Security . . ."

"But why?" Autry asked. "What's going on in L.A. that you guys are so busy? A movie premiere?"

Weir ignored the barb and took a long drag of his cigarette. "Ever hear of the WTO?" he asked.

"The new baseball league?" McCune replied innocently.

Weir shook his head. "No—it's the World Trade Organization. Basically it's a club for the leaders of the wealthiest countries in the world. They get together every other year under the excuse of trying to help the poorest nations with things like feeding the hungry, easing the Third World debt and all that bullshit, but really, it's a powwow on how the megarich can get megaricher."

McCune just shrugged. He was perpetually broke. "No wonder I've never heard of it."

Autry had, however. But he couldn't guess how a WTO meeting was related to the bizarre disappearance of the Coast Guard cutter.

Weir anticipated his question.

"This year, it's the U.S.'s turn to host this WTO shindig," he explained. "They're meeting in Los Angeles. In Beverly Hills, in fact. Starting today, ending tomorrow—or at least the political part of it is."

Weir took another drag on his cigarette, then went on: "Now even though this particular confab is only going to last a day, from a security point of view it's already a fucking nightmare. And this is why: No matter where or when these WTO meetings are held, a ton of protesters show up and do everything they can to bust it up. Who are they? Anarchists, people opposed to one world government, assorted wackos. But also poor farmers from around the world who are sick of getting screwed over by the big rich countries. They gather together and do their best to disrupt these meetings. And frankly, sometimes they almost succeed. I mean, not only have they been active at almost every major WTO meeting, they nearly tore Seattle apart a few years ago when it was held there. Montreal too."

Another drag from his cigarette. "Now, normally, the LAPD is like a little army unto itself. They're highly trained to handle just about anything."

He called up a satellite photo of L.A. on his laptop.

"But for this thing?" he went on. "They'll be stretched real thin. They'll help us out a little bit with the heads of state's own security. But there's only so much they can do when their primary concern will be the protesters. But we also have to worry about terrorists, as this meeting has been publicized for months. That's why my bosses have their undershorts in a bunch these days."

Weir sipped his coffee again. "Now, to further complicate things, this year the administration has decided to put on a real dog and pony show for the leaders of the other nations. So, just before the meeting officially begins, a nuclear sub off L.A. is going to launch a missile that will actually go into orbit—a first for a sub-launched vehicle. The foreign leaders will watch it all on a big screen TV. Should be quite a show.

"Right after that, there is to be a fly-by of the top secret Aurora spy plane. You've heard of this thing, right? It's ramjet-powered, it can reach speeds of 3,000 knots, maybe even 4,000, or even more, depending on who you want to believe. Everyone knows this aircraft exists—but again, when these foreign WTO guys see it for real, they'll be in awe, I guess. Or at least that's the thinking.

"And the third ring of this circus? Well, I don't know all the details yet. But it's going to be a real doozy. So, believe me, security has to be extra tight."

With that, Weir finally finished his coffee. McCune went to refill his cup from the Chinook's always brewing pot, but the agent shook his head no. "I've got to slow down," he said. "I've been pounding this stuff for the past five days. I've got no sleep, nothing good to eat."

But as he was saying this, he reconsidered and signaled McCune that yes, he wanted more.

"I have a stupid question," McCune said, pouring the last of the coffee into Weir's paper cup. "Why are we showing these foreign dudes all our best stuff? I don't know from this sub-shooting thing, but isn't that Aurora plane really top secret?"

Weir was about to launch into an explanation of how flexing one's military muscle to the right people at the right time could pay dividends politics-wise, somewhere down the road.

But Mungo beat him to the punch. And he was infinitely more succinct.

"It's about who has the biggest dick," the stone-faced officer interjected. "That's the only way they can show off these days."

The other three were stunned to hear Mungo's words. Weir, however, saluted him crisply. "Well said, Captain . . ."

Then the CIA man lit yet another cigarette. "So, why am I telling you all this? Because I've been named chief security officer for this WTO meeting. This means I have to be the CIA's boots on the ground at the meeting site itself. The problem is, I've *also* been assigned to look into this Coast Guard thing. But frankly, it's just *too weird* for me or anyone else to think about right now. Bottom line: We can't let anything screw up this WTO meeting."

"So?" Autry prompted him.

"So, I'd like you to check out this Coast Guard

thing for me," he said. "Because your copters have all that excellent interconnected tracking gear, look-down imaging radar stuff, you could maybe find something everyone else missed. Plus, you guys are so secret, no one will know you're involved."

Another cigarette lit, gulp of coffee; Weir went on anxiously.

"Now the CG is of the mind that their ship was hit by a rogue wave and sunk. That's the only thing that makes sense to them, especially with some of the wave heights that had been reported out there. But they don't know about the Galaxy Net; and they don't know what I've just shown you. We can't show it to them, because it is illegal to disseminate any information from or about the G-Net, even to members of our own services, without presidential authority, and believe me, he ain't giving it to them. That means it's up to people privy to the Galaxy Net to determine what really happened."

He dragged on his cigarette again.

"That's why I need you guys," he said. "You've got to get out there and *retrieve* some wreckage, some evidence. A life jacket, piece of burned rubber or metal. Something. *Anything*. All they need is a scrap and they'll be able to tell what the hell happened to that Coast Guard boat. Whether it was sunk by a monster wave—or by 'means unknown.' "

Finally he finished his cigarette, then handed Autry

a packet full of maps, photographs, and further information for the Galaxy Net. "Twenty-four hours," he said. "That's all I need. If you can buy me that much time, then the whole WTO road show flies away and becomes someone else's problem—and then we really see what's up with this."

He checked his watch. It was now 0800 hours. He crushed his coffee cup, stood up and headed out of the helicopter.

Autry stopped him for a moment. He was still holding his set of orders, now ripped in two.

"But are you sure about this?" he asked Weir, displaying the torn orders. "These came right from the top."

They were old friends, so again it was mandatory that they be straight with each other.

"Trust me," Weir said, taking the orders again and tearing them into even smaller pieces. "No matter what Mother Shaw told you, *this* is more important."

With that, he sprinted out to his copter. Thirty seconds later he was gone, his tricked-out aircraft speeding into the west.

"So much for being retired," McCune said.

Mungo's face was screwed up in thought. He looked at Shaw's torn orders. "Does Weir have the authority to do this, Colonel?"

Autry was watching the CIA copter disappear over the stormy horizon to the west. The unit had been given a reprieve to check out little more than a glitch. But that was OK with him. His heart was beating again.

"Can he really do this?" Autry repeated, imagining he could see a slight break in the clouds ahead. "I've got no idea."

CHAPTER 3

X-BATTALION WAS GONE TEN MINUTES LATER.

Bivouac secured, rotors turning, the dozen helicopters lifted out of the NTC without so much as a courtesy call to Fort Irwin's air traffic controllers. By habit alone, they never wanted anyone knowing their movements, and that was especially true this morning. So as soon as they were airborne, they put themselves into a tight diamond pattern and then went down to the deck. At just twenty-five feet off the ground, they turned as one and headed west. The Pacific Ocean was just forty miles away.

The unit flew three types of helicopter. Six UH-60 Black Hawk airframes made up half of the force—but these aircraft were Black Hawks in name only. Each boasted a stretched and fattened fuselage, this to carry more weapons, more gear, bigger engines and more fuel. Oversized by a factor of ten percent, it gave the rugged helicopter an oddly sleeker, almost futuristic look.

Four of these six Black Hawks were designed as flying troop trucks—each could carry up to twenty-two men or several tons of equipment. The remaining pair of UH-60s were called DAPs—Direct Action Penetrators. Translation: pure gunships. Where the flying troop trucks carried weapons in their noses as well as in their cargo bay doors, the DAPs were really loaded for bear. They boasted two 30mm cannon in their noses and four 50-caliber machine guns mounted inside the airframe on either side of the cockpit. They also had stubby wings growing out of their fuselages next to the cargo bays. Everything from antitank missiles, to huge cannon pods, to weapons points for smart weapons, could be found here, along with gigantic fuel tanks which gave the DAPs extended range.

XBat also flew four huge CH-47 Chinooks, a copter almost twice the size of the unit's Black Hawks. The long banana-shaped Chinooks could carry up to twenty tons of stuff, be it weapons, ammo, supplies or soldiers. The Chinooks were also outfitted as heavy gunships with cannons in the nose and near each cargo bay door, plus twin 50-caliber machine guns attached to the rear deck, weapons that could be fired, even in flight, when the copter's rear ramp was lowered.

The last two XBat aircraft were the odd buglike AH-6s. These aircraft were not much bigger than a minivan. Yet they were swift and silent, and, with formidable cannons in their noses, deadly as well.

But the dozen copters were more than a bunch of

aerial weapons platforms. One of the Chinooks—the command copter—carried almost as much airborne warning gear as the famous AWACs plane used by the U.S. Air Force. The command ship also featured a vast communications suite, a substantial eavesdropping capability, plus equipment to conduct search and rescue operations.

It also served as the unit's connection to the dysfunctional Galaxy Net—its one drawback. Most of XBat's surveillance and navigation gear was designed to work in sync with the G-Net. When everything was running right, it could be an infallible tool in fighting the bad guys.

But in truth, sometimes the G-Net was more trouble than it was worth.

XBAT REACHED THE PACIFIC FIFTEEN MINUTES LATER.

Once over open water, the dozen copters loosened their formation and turned northwest. The last known location of the Coast Guard cutter *Steadfast* was about seventy miles off the California coast, at a point roughly halfway between Los Angeles and San Diego. It would take XBat another twenty minutes to reach this area.

The gigantic storm was still churning up the Pacific, this its ninth day. The tempest was now right ahead of them, seemingly locked in place by monstrous winds. Flying in the lead DAP, Autry once again contemplated the threatening gray mass; it looked like an impossibly huge mountain, miles long, miles high, with no way to fly over it or under it. It was like something from a bad dream.

But this time Autry didn't dwell on what the storm clouds meant for him. Rather, he saw them as just as foreboding for the rest of XBat. Before taking off from the NTC, he'd gathered his men around and told them the rest of the news Shaw had given him: that the unit was not only breaking up, but was being completely dissolved. Everybody within was being let go by the military.

The men were plainly shocked. First, they learn the unit was being disbanded, now they found out they were being fired as well. Autry allowed them a few moments to regain their composure. Then he told them about Weir's dilemma, how they were needed one last time, and how this search mission took precedent over what the shortsighted types in Washington had ordered them to do. The mood changed. The men saw the cutter mission for what it was: one more day to live. But it was such a strange situation, Autry had to ask the tough question: Was there anyone who wanted to stay behind? To pass on this one last flight? If so, he should make himself known.

But no one raised their hand.

Not even Mungo.

THE TWELVE COPTERS PLUNGED INTO THE STORM LIKE the tip of an arrow. It was suddenly as dark as night and the winds started violently throwing around the high-tech helicopters. No sane copter pilot would ever think of going into this maelstrom, yet this was just the kind of hazardous flying that all of TF-160 trained for. Through raw experience alone, Autry's team were experts at it.

Using their advanced navigation systems, they soon found the point where the Coast Guard cutter was last seen. Though it was raining like hell and the wind was still fierce, the seas around the target area were strangely calm. There was no wreckage here, though. No sign that anything untoward had happened at all.

The unit began to circle. The Coast Guard's own search teams had scoured this area for two days and found nothing. They'd reluctantly left the area hours before, braving the weather, but finally giving up their comrades for dead.

Now it was XBat's turn. While its primary mission was about retrieving any wreckage that would either blame or clear the top-secret Galaxy Net in the mishap, this search was also about the lives of the cutter's crew and the civilians riding with them. The human factor of this tragedy had gotten lost a bit in the storm, but close to eighty people were gone.

On Autry's call, the twelve helicopters ceased their orbits. With the precision of an aerobatic team, each copter banked into a hover and slowly aligned itself with a different point on the compass.

"Remember, boys," Autry told them now. "No risks.

No heroes. Everyone stay safe. Officially, we're out here looking for some wreckage, and nothing more."

With that, he gave the order and the copters streaked off in twelve different directions.

Eyes peeled, their radar imaging gear turned up to full power, they commenced their search.

Seventy miles away

Gary Weir was at 10,000 feet and descending toward Los Angeles.

His all-black Bell Textron helicopter was running hot-rod smooth, as always. His pilot, an Air America veteran code-named Alberto, was extraordinary. One of the best pilots the Agency employed, he'd done covert missions on every continent, including both poles. Word was he could fly a copter through a pinhole without scraping the paint. He was also smart enough to keep the chatter to a minimum on their trips together, letting Weir do what he did best: think.

It was now 0800. The sky over LA was cloudy in spots, but mostly bright blue, with a blazing morning sun. The water off Los Angeles looked almost aqua, this because the huge offshore storm was still churning up the shoreline. Weir had never seen the ocean that color before.

They came down on the city itself. There was a strange haze hovering over downtown; weirdly, it too had an aqua glow. They leveled off over Santa Monica

Beach, and it was here, in the parking lots along the sea walls, that they first saw the crowds forming below.

All the activity looked like the Rose Bowl parade about to kick off. Several thousand people were milling around the Wilshire area, banners fluttering in the breeze, streamers hanging from light posts and palm trees. Even fireworks, apparently, red streaks of light shooting up into the sky. Weir sensed a festive vibe coming up from the crowd below.

That is, until he realized that the banners were American flags, cut to pieces or turned upside down. And the streamers were really bedsheets painted into signs denouncing all things American. And the fireworks? Signal flares, shot from flare guns. This was no parade. This was a swarm of protesters ready to march to the WTO meeting site.

At Weir's request, Alberto flew lower and slower. They saw more people gathered along the roads running up from the beach, with more upside-down flags and anti-American signs rippling in the breeze. Some below had strangely painted faces. Others were wearing battle helmets. Many had red kerchiefs pulled over their faces. Many had gas masks. There had to be at least 20,000 of them, stretched for two miles along the beach area. It was as if they'd appeared out of nowhere. All of them looked ready for battle.

Just a few blocks away, where Wilshire crossed Santa Monica Boulevard, another army was forming. Long lines of black and white assault vehicles, even longer columns of heavily armed figures in heavy black riot gear. This was the LAPD. At just about 15,000, their numbers were smaller than the protesters, but they appeared much better prepared. Their line stretched for more than a mile along Santa Monica; they'd also sealed off many city blocks in all directions.

Behind the swarm of police was a rolling cavalcade of media trucks. Sprouting movable forests of satellite dishes, and moving amid ribbons of thick electrical wire running everywhere, they were ready to record whatever would unfold when the two armies collided, which at this point seemed inevitable.

Weir took it all in then slumped back into his seat.

This is going to be a *long* day, he thought.

A PARTICULARLY LARGE GROUP OF DEMONSTRATORS was gathered in the huge public parking lot near the corner of West Wilshire Boulevard and Santa Monica Beach Road.

There were more than a thousand protesters on hand here, mostly kids in their twenties, students, artists, the genially underemployed. Most had something—a rag, a painted face or kerchief—with which to hide their features. Torn American flags and anti-WTO signs abounded. Some protesters were warming up their vocal cords with their best anti-U.S. chants. Others were stacking baseball bats and pieces of rebar.

Despite all this, there was an almost circuslike atmosphere around the parking lot. Some of the kids were playing hacky-sack. Some were getting high. Many were eating totally organic breakfasts bought from the Earth Mother take-out food truck parked nearby.

There was a round of applause when the sun broke through the last of the clouds. The sky was clear now, except to the west. Fifty miles out into the Pacific, the storm was still raging.

Most of the protesters had arrived in buses provided by the plethora of anarchist and free world protest groups. Others had walked, or ridden bicycles to the gathering point. Most of them had sense enough not to bring their cars anywhere near the protest site. That was just begging for a tow job and riot club through the windshield.

That's why it caught some of their attention when five all-white Ford SUVs suddenly appeared on the edge of the vast parking lot. Someone yelled: "It's the UN!" And indeed the vehicles looked governmental in that plain white, no-frills sort of way.

Truth was, the SUVs were stolen.

They slowly made their way through the sea of milling protesters, entering the parking lot itself and finally coming to a stop in the almost empty north end. There were five men in each SUV. Unlike many of the protesters, these men appeared clean and recently bathed, with neatly trimmed haircuts and combat boots instead of old sneakers.

Their appearance made some curious. A few protesters wandered over to where the SUVs were parked, but the men ignored them. Instead, they went about unloading their trucks. Each man retrieved two large olive-drab canvas sacks and a wooden box marked AIR FREIGHT. The wooden boxes were about the size of a six-pack of beer.

In fact, there were six items within the wooden boxes, but they were not brewskis. They were high explosive fragmentation grenades. And in their sacks, almost fifty pounds of belt ammunition each.

Each SUV had also been carrying a coffin-size wooden box on its roof. These too were stenciled AIR FREIGHT. The boxes were now retrieved and opened in full view of the gawking protesters. Inside were AK-47 assault rifles. Each man took one.

The protesters were surprised, to say the least, to see the heavy weaponry. But they were confused as well. The men were unpacking the combat rifles with such nonchalance, there didn't seem to be anything to get too upset about.

A few protesters went, "Wow . . ." And one kid yelled from the back: "Hey man, it's illegal to carry a rifle in Los Angeles."

To this, one of the men looked up and smiled. "What are you going to do? Call a cop?"

With that, the two dozen men all put on ski masks and then tied red kerchiefs over their faces as well. Again, many of the protesters were wearing, or were planning to wear, ski masks once the demonstration started. And most of those that weren't would be wearing a red kerchief to hide their faces.

But these guys were wearing both.

Face coverings in place, the masked men very casually walked away, making no attempt to hide their heavy weapons. They turned up Cyprus Avenue and disappeared into an even larger crowd swelling there.

Those protesters who'd witnessed all this remained confused. Most were sure the men were cops. But a few of the more radical ones saw something different.

"Oh, man," one said to no one in particular. "This is *really* gonna rock and roll."

MEANWHILE, WEIR'S TEXTRON FLEW ON.

Over Sunset Boulevard, along the edge of West Hollywood, swinging back to the north side of Beverly Hills. Ahead was an area called La Brea Heights. This was about as exclusive as L.A. got. There was a huge, resort here called the Briar Patch. It was a place that only the richest of the rich ever got to see.

The resort's main building featured a futuristic, flying saucer design. Conference rooms and a large meeting hall were contained within. Surrounded by a very private golf course, the landscape was a patchwork of bright green fairways, emerald forests, and water hazards the sizes of small oceans.

There was an army down there too—except you could not see this one. At least not flying over it. Private security people, many of them ex-military, were stationed in the glens, in the roughs, even in the water holes, manning nearly invisible positions. They were all armed to the teeth. The woods bordering the resort were festooned with hundreds of security cameras and other silent detection devices. Visible security patrols were constantly moving about the square-mile resort property in jeeps and ATVs. There were also a couple dozen undercover security personnel in position inside the resort, ready for anything.

Precautions were always in place whenever a special event was happening at the Briar Patch. But what was scheduled here today was far from routine. This was where the WTO would be meeting. Within the hour, the leaders of the world's ten wealthiest nations, plus their entourages, would be arriving at Briar Patch.

Because of this, the resort's private security people would be supplemented by members of the Secret Service, State Department Security, the Federal Protection Service, and the FBI. Thus, the security force within Briar Patch had swelled to more than 200, while outside its perimeter the LAPD had mobilized another 5,000 police officers, all of them trained in riot containment, SWAT tactics and crowd control. On this strange aqua morning, the ultraexclusive resort had been turned into an armed camp.

Weir flew right over the resort and then over the Hollywood Hills beyond. They were down to 750 feet and flying fast. Moving by at a blur, the terrain below quickly changed from opulence to squalor. Within a minute they were approaching a particularly run-down section of L.A. known as Northeast Central.

This place made Watts look inviting. Blocks of worn-down housing and burned-out buildings. Abandoned cars were everywhere. In the middle of it all, a huge cemetery, a haven for drug addicts and gang members. It looked more like a battlefield than a place of rest.

The copter passed over the intersection of Sunrise Avenue and Vineyard. These four corners were collectively known as the most dangerous place in America; murders, drive-by shootings and vicious gang-banging happened here both day and night.

On the edge of this hot urban morass was a small, long-ago abandoned airfield. It was a place where some movie stars and studio moguls kept their private planes before Northeast Central fell into decay in the fifties. Weir's copter circled its single runway once, then set down. Weir climbed out and checked his watch. It was 8:25 A.M. Weir told his pilot to keep the rotors turning. Then he set out, walking over the cracked concrete.

A minute later he was standing at the notorious intersection of Vineyard and Sunrise. Spent shell casings littered the sidewalk, the smell of gunpowder in the morning air. A cab pulled up right on cue. The driver nodded at Weir and then tapped his dashboard three times. Weir climbed into the back of the beat-up sedan.

The driver listened to his directions. In two minutes

they arrived in front of a run-down motel about a mile from the old airport. This was the Willows Canyon Inn and it was barely standing. Pockmarked and crumbling, every window in the place was either broken or boarded up. Weir had seen better lodgings in downtown Falluja, and that was *after* the battle.

He checked the 45-caliber pistol he always carried with him. The clip was full. He tapped the back of the cab's seat three times then climbed out. The cab screeched away in a cloud of dust and litter.

Weir walked through the fleabag's parking lot, hypodermic needles crunching beneath his feet. Empty liquor bottles and hundreds of empty crack bags were strewn everywhere. He climbed the rusty, exterior staircase, found Room 1313 and knocked twice. The door opened; a familiar face was within. He was a short, round man in his fifties, red-nosed and hairy everywhere except atop his bullet-shaped head. This was Denny Dana, a veteran CIA street operative. Weir had known him for years.

They shook hands. "Are you the one responsible for booking me into this dump?" Dana asked him. "If so, I'll have to beat your ass."

"It was necessary," Weir told him, looking around the room. More than a few homicides had been committed here. "We wanted your trail to be as cold as possible. Staying here for the past few nights did the trick."

Weir got down to business. "So? Are you ready for this?" he asked.

Dana shrugged good-naturedly. "Piece of cake," he said. "Get in, look around. Keep everyone in line. Call in the cavalry if we hit a bump. A nice easy one for my last mission."

"Last mission?" Weir was surprised to hear this. "You're going someplace?"

Dana nodded. "Yep—it's called 'early retirement.' I've been with the agency twenty-three years, and now they tell me they don't have enough money to keep side men like me around. So they made me an offer I couldn't refuse. The wife and I are moving up to Cape Cod and I'm going to watch the tide go in and out for a while."

Weir thought he was kidding. No money? The Agency depended on guys like Dana—ordinary looking blokes who could eyeball sensitive places—or potential targets—without ever raising a fuss. Letting someone like him go was like clamping off a crucial part of the Agency's blood flow.

"They just figured I was getting too old for this crap," Dana went on. "And you are too, my friend. They'll be dropping the same thing on you any day now. And you know, like that TV show *Deal or No Deal*? Believe me, when your time comes, take the money and run, man. That's what I'm doing—more for my own peace of mind than anything else. I just can't take these guys who are running things in Washington anymore."

Weir was nearly speechless. Early retirement? For him? He didn't even want to think about it. He quickly changed back to the subject at hand.

He passed Dana a credit card, a cell phone, and a bottle of hair dye. "Here are your tools, man—and you better start hustling. You've got to be on your way in less than an hour."

Dana looked at the hair dye. "Blond?" he protested. "You want me to go *blond* for this job?"

"Just highlights," Weir replied in all seriousness. "There's instructions on the label telling you how to do it. It's the style for where you are going. Everyone has to have a 'look' or you'll be tagged right away as being out of place."

"Everyone? A 'look'?" Dana repeated mockingly. "Even short, fat dumpy middle-aged guys?"

Weir patted him on the back.

"*Especially* them," he said.

WEIR LEFT THE ROOM AND WENT TO THE MOTEL MANager's office. He found the clerk sitting behind a thick bulletproof partition reading a *Gent* magazine.

The clerk gave Weir the once-over. "I was expecting you earlier," he said.

"I'm running late," Weir replied. "Which is why I can't stay and chat. I'm just checking that everything's OK."

On the wall behind the clerk was a bank of video monitors; all of them were attached to small hidden cameras in Room 1313. Their purpose was to keep a safe eye on Agent Denny Dana, as at the moment he was one of the most valuable CIA assets in L.A. The clerk, also an Agency operative, was in charge of watching over him.

Weir indicated the video monitors and said, "You know your assignment then, right? Make sure no one bothers our friend there, so he can get to where he has to go. *Capeesh?*"

The hotel clerk nodded once, then he went back to his *Gent*.

"*Capeesh,*" he said.

CHAPTER 4

Colder, Arizona

THE SALOON WAS CALLED THE DROP DEAD INN.

It was an appropriate name. The place was small and creepy, just like the town of Colder, population thirty-one. Made of mud brick and cracked adobe, the saloon held just a few tables, a few stools and a dingy bramble pine bar. Only beer and tequila were served here, both at room temperature. Unlike other drinking places in Arizona, pistols didn't have to be checked at the door.

It was now eight-thirty in the morning. Four people were in the saloon. Two were Ipacho Indians; they'd been passed out since midnight. The bartender was also asleep, snoring away in a chair in the corner. On a hotplate next to him, a rusty pan full of burnt chili was slowly beginning to boil over.

The fourth man was sitting at the bar drinking tap water, which in this place was as dangerous as the tequila. He was Davis Smith. Mid-forties, buzz cut, but showing signs of gray, at one time Smith was one of the U.S. military's best test pilots. He'd spent fifteen years splitting his time between Edwards Air Force Base in California and Area 51 in Nevada flying top-secret aircraft. He'd attained the rank of colonel at a very young age, and at one time had more hours logged in the air than any other U.S. test pilot. And because in some cases he was being paid by both the government and the airplane manufacturers, he was one of the wealthiest people in his profession as well.

Or he had been, until two years ago. That's when his storybook career came tumbling down. It began as a slow but steady drip. While he'd never experienced a major crash while testing new designs, he'd been in a few minor crack-ups. One fucked up his knees, another had broken his left shoulder. Both times the Air Force docs failed to put him back together correctly, which led to joint pain that would have disabled lesser men. But as these things didn't affect his flying at first, the military let him keep on testing airplanes. As he got older, though, and the aches and pains became greater, he began medicating himself, first with alcohol, then prescription painkillers. It didn't take long for him to be flying high every waking moment of the day.

This drug abuse changed his personality—it always does. In an effort to replace the adrenaline high he'd gotten from test flights earlier in his career, he began gambling. The problem was, he was as bad a gambler as he was a good test pilot. Thousands began going down the drain. He spent more time away from his wife and kids, and more time getting drunk in the casinos in Vegas. In less than a year, his life's savings disappeared. A nasty divorce followed, with an embarrassing bankruptcy case close behind.

Hiding all this from the military was a major endeavor, but an Air Force shrink finally caught on—test pilots with personal problems were nothing new. He arranged for Smith to take a six-month leave of absence, along with a promise that his career would be waiting for him, intact, when he returned.

Trouble was, the shrink lied. Though Smith straightened himself out in that half year, when he returned to service he'd discovered that younger, more sober test pilots had leapfrogged over him. All available test planes already had their pilots and support crews and sponsors. Smith had nothing. It took him about a month to realize his career of testing X-planes was over.

The Air Force didn't drop him completely. He was reduced in rank to second lieutenant and liasoned to the Arizona Air National Guard, where his pay rate was cut to one-tenth his previous salary. He began drinking again, and then the gambling came back. He was soon more heavily in debt than ever before. And this time the people he owed money to weren't exactly Boy Scouts.

Part of his vice was playing poker online, a real haven for fools. Some of the regular players heard him griping about his recent crash dive. A mysterious phone call followed; within it was a proposition for Smith to earn enough money to kiss off the military and pay off his debts ten times over.

That's why he was here today, in The Drop Dead Inn, with both his knees and his shoulder causing him so much pain he could barely move.

He'd just finished his glass of cloudy water when two people stumbled into the bar. The mysterious phone call had told Smith to expect "hippies," and this pair fit the bill. Both were in their twenties, wearing T-shirts, filthy jeans and appalling flip-flops. They hadn't bathed in weeks. One was giggling madly, the other appeared terrified. Both looked stoned.

They spied the passed-out Indians and the dozing bartender, then turned their attention to Smith. He looked at them like a person looked at road kill. He just shook his head and felt all the air run out of him.

How could he have sunk this low? he wondered.

THE MEETING LASTED ONLY TEN MINUTES.

The strangers were mostly interested in what kind of airplane Smith flew these days, checking whatever he told them against notes someone named "Douglas" had scrawled on a sheet of paper for them. Smith explained he was not driving top-of-the-line fighters anymore. Just the opposite. His current plane was the A-10 Thunderbolt, probably the least glamorous aircraft in the Air Force's inventory. It was a stubby-nosed attack plane that could barely top 300 knots and resembled a bathtub with wings. Still, the scrubs asked many questions about the airplane. Exactly what weapons did it carry? How low could it fly? Could it be shot down by something like a hunting rifle?

Smith gave them every answer as best he could, all the while wanting to get as far away from the pair as possible. After a few more details were discussed, they were finally done. Except for one last question.

The guy who seemed more stoned, and not terrified, asked him: "Are you really ready to do this, man? You sure you got the intestinal fortitude?" His eyes were glassy and bright red.

Smith was instantly pissed. "Just show me the goddamn money," he spit back at him. "And hurry up. I have to be in the preflight in two hours."

Chastened, the stoner opened his dirty knapsack. Inside were hundreds of crisp thousand-dollar bills.

"Two million," the punk told him. "Enough for you to pay off your little problem and take off for good. This kind of scratch goes a long way down in the islands."

Smith fought off a smile. Could these two be *that* dopey? Would they be stupid enough to actually give him this money—with no guarantee that he would do what they wanted him to do?

No, the scruffs weren't brain-dead, not quite. Because as Mr. Red Eyes handed the knapsack to Smith, the other one nervously passed him a brown manila envelope. It too had the name "Douglas" written on it.

Smith opened it to find a handful of eight-by-ten photographs. Obviously taken through a telephoto lens, they showed Smith's kids going in and out of their house in Tucson, walking to school, playing in their backyard.

"Keep those," the head punk told him. "Just in case you start thinking about screwing with us, they might make you think again."

With that, the pair gave him a mock salute and went out the door with a laugh.

CHAPTER 5

X-Battalion
Eighty miles off shore

"EVER HEAR OF Q-SHIPS, COLONEL?"

Bobby Autry was busy transferring fuel from his reserves to his main tanks when he heard the question. It was his copilot, WSO Zucker, doing the asking.

"Q-Ships?" Autry replied, turning his eyes away from the fuel panel and back to the enormous expanse of the angry Pacific below him. "I'm not sure . . ."

They'd been out here for thirty minutes now, flying their south-southwest search pattern, but with zero results. The weather was still rough; the rain was particularly brutal. At times it was like flying through a car wash. A very *bumpy* car wash. All the while, they'd been straining their eyes trying to spot anything on the surface remaining from the doomed Coast Guard cutter, this as their look-down radars were doing huge electronic sweeps of the area.

Typically, then, the mission had been both intense and boring. Never adverse to idle chatter, Zucker—who was lucky to be alive after suffering a near fatal wound during their Venezuela adventure—was trying to pass the time.

"The Germans used Q-Ships during World War Two," he explained. "They were commerce raiders, ordinary cargo ships that were secretly armed with all kinds of heavy weapons. The German navy would sail them off the beaten track, like in the Indian Ocean, or off West Africa. They'd cozy up to some unsuspecting Allied freighter and then, boom! They'd lower their disguise and start blasting away. Very effective tactic for picking off ships, one at a time."

"And you're telling me this because . . . ?" Autry asked him.

"Because finding the Q-Ships was one of the hardest things the Allies had to do in World War Two," Zucker replied, scanning the seas on his side of the copter. "They could almost hide in plain sight because the ocean—*any* ocean—is so big."

Autry couldn't disagree. Even under the best conditions, open-sea searches were always difficult, simply because the spaces involved were always so vast. That's why, as the minutes ticked by, he was beginning to lose faith in this mission. Looking for wayward ships on the wide ocean was bad enough. Trying to spot pieces of debris on that same wide ocean was infinitely harder.

Autry's eyes went back to his fuel panel, second nature for any copter pilot. Fuel would soon become a factor for them. Though all of XBat's aircraft had extended range capability, they couldn't fly around out here forever.

"Strange, though," Zucker sighed. "Us out here, looking for wreckage. After everything we've done, it's a weird way to end our careers."

That's when their radio came to life.

It was a message from Lieutenant Ozzo, the pilot of one of XBat's flying troop trucks. One look at his situation readout screen told Autry that Ozzo's copter was doing a search pattern about twenty miles off Venice Beach, way in the other direction.

Ozzo spoke a code word, his way of requesting that they go on a secure, scrambled radio channel. Autry complied, punching a pair of buttons on his communication set. He quickly picked up Ozzo's signal again.

"What's up, Lieutenant?" Autry asked him.

"I think we found something, Colonel . . ." Ozzo replied.

Autry looked over at Zucker; he was as surprised as Autry to hear the message.

Autry keyed his chin mic. "You mean you've found the cutter?" he asked Ozzo.

"No, sir," was the reply. "We found the two cargo ships."

*　　　*　　　*

OZZO'S WORDS IMMEDIATELY BEGAN SPINNING around Autry's head. They found the cargo ships? The ones on hand for the Coast Guard cutter's demise? With everyone concentrating on locating the cutter's wreckage, this was the last thing anyone expected to hear.

Just like that, the dynamics of the search changed. Though he couldn't imagine where they'd been in the last forty-eight hours, finding the cargo ships might have been the next best thing to finding the cutter itself. At the very least, someone had to talk to the crews on the two ships.

"Do you have these vessels in visual contact right now?" Autry called back to Ozzo.

Strangely, there was no reply.

Autry repeated the message. "Do you have visual and what is your exact location?"

Still nothing.

"Is he still on the scrambler?" Autry asked Zucker.

The young copilot began pushing buttons and changing frequencies. He went up and down all the scrambled channels, switched back to the regular radio bands and then back to the scrambles again.

But it was no use.

They couldn't get Ozzo back on the line.

"Well, *this* is a little nuts," Zucker deadpanned.

Autry immediately rotated his controls 180 degrees, turning the Black Hawk on a dime. In seconds they were screaming along at 200 knots, heading for Ozzo's position. At the same time, he told Zucker to call the rest of the unit and have them do the same thing. Suddenly something was very wrong here.

A flurry of radio activity enveloped XBat. Every copter broke off its search pattern and was quickly speeding to Ozzo's location. But this would not be a quick thing. Again, Ozzo's copter had been searching just off the coast of L.A., flying on the edges of the storm but still in thick fog and deluging rain.

It was XBat's bad luck that his copter was as far away from the rest of them as possible.

IT TOOK SIXTEEN MINUTES FOR THE FIRST COPTERS to reach Ozzo's last known location. They found nothing. No sign of Ozzo or his five-man crew. No sign of the two cargo ships. Nothing but the stormy sea.

Autry was soon on the scene, frantically scouring the ocean in every direction. His worst fear was his craziest: that the Galaxy Net had somehow shot down Ozzo's helicopter. Yet his gut told him something else was going on here.

Los Angeles was just over the horizon. The rising sun was illuminating the tallest buildings in its skyline. And instead of an open empty ocean, the XBat pilots now found a rather crowded waterway to the east, just beyond the mist and rain. Because they were so close to coastline, they could see more than two dozen cargo ships moving nearby. All of them were heading to or away from the massive cargo unloading facility known as the Port of L.A.

Autry checked his watch. Eighteen minutes had passed since Ozzo's call had reached them, enough time for a cargo ship to sail at least a mile, maybe more. He looked at the traffic jam of ships just a few thousand yards to the south.

At full speed, an empty cargo ship might have even entered the Port of Los Angeles by this time.

So how could he find out what happened here?

"We can always ask the G-Net, sir," Zucker reminded him.

This was true. With its huge memory banks holding billions of images taken from space every minute, the G-Net could also look into the past, locate an incident and drag it up into the present.

But was it sober today? Would its readings be accurate?

Autry knew they had to take the chance. He called over to McCune's Chinook. This was the aircraft that carried the bulk of the unit's Galaxy Net equipment. McCune was adept at conversing with the complicated spy system and divining what it said back to them. That's why he flew this command aircraft.

"Can you get a read-down on this area for about eighteen minutes ago?" Autry asked him.

"I can try," McCune responded. "But it might take a while."

The next two minutes went by with agonizing slowness. Autry and the others continued their desperate orbital search patterns. The two small AH-6s were running so close to the water, the waves were crashing against the bottom of their landing struts.

Finally McCune came back on the line.

"I've got something, Colonel," he reported. "Or, at least I think I do . . ."

McCune transmitted the G-Net's findings directly to Autry's control panel TV screen. The spy system had come up with a video capture of the area less than twenty minutes before. Looking down from space through a yellowed haze, it showed what looked to be the same pair of battered cargo ships, still sailing together, heading south, with Ozzo's copter beginning to circle in behind them.

On Autry's suggestion, Zucker called up the original G-Net images from the night the cutter disappeared.

"Those are definitely the same cargo ships, sir," Zucker confirmed. "See? One has a red stack, the other's dull yellow."

Autry compared the two images and agreed. They were a match.

They watched now as Ozzo's copter went down low and slow and began a long pass between the ships. Suddenly, a streak of fire erupted from one freighter. There was a trail of smoke, and a bright flash seen on top of Ozzo's rotor cap. As this was happening, another spit of flame shot out of the second freighter, hitting the copter on its tail. Twin explosions obscured the video for the next few seconds. When it came back on, the copter was gone.

Autry stared at the TV screen. Did he just see that?

"Is this thing working right?" he roared back to McCune. "Or are we looking at another G-Net wet dream?"

"This clip is registering as a real event," McCune responded, trying to stay cool. "Everything is telling us this *really* happened."

But Autry didn't want to believe it—because it was just dawning on him what fools they'd been. Distracted by the immense technology of the Galaxy Net, as well as the weirdness of the big storm itself, they'd failed to consider a third possibility about what might have happened to the *Steadfast*. But it was crystal clear now: It wasn't a wave that sank the cutter; nor was it the Galaxy Net. It was these two freighters. They were armed—*heavily* armed—with all kinds of weapons. Just like Q-Ships.

As for Ozzo and his crew?

"Son of a bitch," Autry whispered angrily. "Those assholes *shot* them down . . ."

CHAPTER 6

Thirty minutes later

THERE WERE ONLY TWO POLICE OFFICERS IN THE TINY coastal town of Cliffside, California, and at the moment both were asleep inside their squad car.

The older of the two was Joe Whalen. He was the unofficial chief, father of five, full-time almond grower, part-time cop. Just about everyone in town called him "Chief." The younger man was Alex Ryan. An athletic star during his years at the nearby regional high school, he was Cliffside's deputy by default.

They were parked in an almond field off old California Route 19, just this side of the Cliffside town line. It had been a long night for them. They'd come on duty at noon the day before with special orders to pull a twenty-four-hour shift. They'd been able to grab just one cup of coffee in that time, around 9:00 P.M. They'd spent the rest of the night tired and hungry. And as the air-conditioning in their run-down patrol car rarely worked right, it had been hot and sweaty too.

It was rare for them to be on duty together, never mind doing a twenty-four-hour triple shift. Cliffside's population was less than two hundred, and half of them, artists and the like, only lived there part-time. But because of the huge anti-WTO protests happening up in L.A., forty miles to the north, the Cliffside town council decided that the police would go on round-the-clock alert, just in case some of the trouble spilled south.

This was unlikely—which was good, because the Cliffside PD was woefully unprepared. Both officers were armed only with ancient .38 service revolvers holding just four bullets each. They didn't have a standard police radio in their car, only a cell phone. Nor did they have any direct contact with the LAPD or anyone else up in Los Angeles. Their orders were simple: If they saw any trouble coming Cliffside's way, they were to dial 911 for the Highway Patrol, just like everyone else.

IT WAS NINE-FIFTEEN WHEN WHALEN AND RYAN were rudely awakened.

The cell phone was going off. They were both dazed for a moment, startled that they had fallen asleep. Finally Whalen answered the phone. It was Phil Motoike, owner of the bed-and-breakfast that sat atop of the town's cliff.

Both cops knew Motoike; he was a clear-headed, sensible person. But at the moment he was so flustered he could barely speak. He finally managed to scream that the cops had to get up to the cliff as fast as possible—and then he hung up.

Still sleepy, Whalen pulled the cruiser out onto Route 19 and started climbing the winding dirt road that led up to the cliff. At eighty-three feet high, the grassy cliff provided a wide panoramic view of the mighty Pacific; indeed, it was one of the best ocean views in all of southern California.

The wind began blowing briskly as the cops continued their ascent. Fog banks were still lingering in the area and they had to use their windshield wipers to see. Their air conditioner finally kicked in and the fog on the inside of the car began to go away too. The AC was so loud, though, it obscured any noise coming from outside.

Reaching the halfway point up the hill, the two officers saw a clutch of people standing near the edge of the cliff above, pointing anxiously out to sea. People on the front porch of the B&B were doing the same thing. There were even people hanging out of the windows of the picturesque lodge waving to the cops and urging them on.

Telling Ryan to hang on, the chief floored it, and the car moved a little quicker up the steep hill. They saw more people running up to the cliff from the opposite direction. Some of them were screaming at them, but they couldn't be heard because of the air conditioner.

Finally Ryan killed the AC and rolled down his window. They immediately heard loud noises going off; they sounded like sonic booms.

Stopping about twenty-five feet from the B&B, Whalen and Ryan got out and resumed their climb on foot. The noise was tremendous now, it felt like the air itself was shaking. Some people up on the cliff were screaming. Pistols drawn, the cops pushed their way through the growing crowd and at last reached the top of the cliff.

What they saw was astonishing: a battered old cargo ship, sailing just a few hundred feet off the coast, was being viciously attacked by a swarm of helicopters.

It didn't seem real. There were hundreds of small explosions going off up and down the ship's hull; half of the helicopters were mercilessly raking it back and forth with cannon fire. Other copters were pouring rockets into the stricken vessel. The ship's three masts had been decapitated and its wheelhouse was engulfed in flame. Its deck was being absolutely perforated by the onslaught. The vessel was barely crawling along, an almost pathetic attempt to get away. Warning bells and fire buzzers were going off all over her. Some crewmen were jumping overboard, others were trying to lower a life raft. Smoke was everywhere.

It was savage.

And the helicopters were relentless.

Finally Whalen was able to scream: *"What the hell is going on here?"*

Motoike, the B&B owner, ran up to them. He was out of breath, but still tried to explain: Some of his patrons were out for a morning stroll along the cliff when the old cargo ship came into view. It appeared out of a fog bank very close to the rocky shore. In fact, the people on the cliff thought it was in trouble, as it seemed too close to the shoreline.

That's when the helicopters showed up . . .

They'd come quickly. One moment the cloudy sky was empty, the next it was full of them. At first the copters were moving back and forth, low over the water, as if looking for something. As the copters were obviously military, some witnesses assumed they were part of the security for the anti-WTO demonstrations up in L.A.

But then the copters spotted by the old freighter. They immediately broke up their formation and began circling the ship.

"They started shooting a second later!" Motoike was yelling hoarsely over the noise. "And they haven't stopped since!"

The cops still couldn't believe it. The shock waves alone were incredible; it was like standing too close to a very large out-of-control fireworks display. The damage already done to the freighter was staggering. Huge geysers of flame and smoke were broiling out of her and leaping into the morning sky. All of its masts had been shot down and its control house had been obliterated. The ship was rocking back and forth in the water like it was a toy.

But then Deputy Ryan thought he had an explanation for the improbable sight. "Is someone filming a movie down there?" he asked.

Chief Whalen finally snapped out of his stupor and began dialing the Highway Patrol. But before he hit the first button, there was a tremendous explosion—it was so bright, it blinded them. Everyone on the cliff went down. Some rolled to the bottom of the hill, others just hugged the dirt. More explosions followed. The cliff itself began to shake. Everyone still on top thought it was going to collapse into the sea and take them with it.

But then all the shaking suddenly stopped and it became eerily quiet again. When those on top of the cliff got back to their feet, they looked out to sea to find the old rusty ship was essentially gone. All that remained was a smoking hulk already sunk in the shallow water. The rest of the ship had been blown away.

However, somehow, a handful of its crew had managed to jump ship before it blew up. They were now swimming to shore. But suddenly two of the larger helicopters appeared and with stomach-churning precision opened up on these swimmers, tearing them to pieces before flying away again.

Only one crewman made it to shore. He'd staggered up onto the rocks, out of breath and in shock, when one of the small helicopters came out of nowhere. It fired its nose gun in a whirring fashion, shredding the man until there was nothing left.

That's when Whalen turned to Deputy Ryan and said, "This ain't no movie . . ."

Los Angeles
LAX

Major Jim Shaw emerged from the bright yellow taxi, threw the driver a hundred-dollar bill and told him to keep the change.

Shaw was exhausted. His long ride to the NTC had taken him nearly a day; finding XBat inside the massive training center took almost as long. The ride out had been a dusty, bumpy affair as well.

But now his job was done; the Pentagon's Grim Reaper had struck again. It was time to head back for Washington and sleep for a couple weeks. Or more.

He'd caught a quick military flight out of Fort Irwin; it deposited him at the old L.A. Airport. The expensive cab ride to LAX followed, paid for by Uncle Sam, and now here he was, with twenty minutes to spare before he boarded his commercial flight back East. His plan was to get a quick bourbon at the airport bar, then have another once the plane lifted off. That was usually enough to knock him out for the flight home.

But this dream came to an abrupt end when, upon entering the terminal, Shaw found two men in bad suits waiting for him.

He let out a groan. These guys were government

agents—he just didn't know who they belonged to. But it really didn't matter.

They approached him, badges cupped in the palms of their hands. California Homeland Security.

"Major Shaw?" one asked.

There was no use fighting it. "Yes?"

"You have to come with us," the second man said, taking Shaw's suitcase from him.

"Why?" Shaw asked him, alarmed.

"There has been an incident, down the coast, about forty-five minutes from here," one explained. "The Pentagon asked us to locate you. Your bosses want you to get down there right away and run some damage control. We have a helicopter waiting. Come this way please?"

A CHP TRAFFIC COPTER TOOK JUST TWENTY MINUTES to whisk Shaw down the coast of California to the town of Cliffside.

He had no idea what was going on, and calls to his superiors in Washington had gone unanswered. Still, one of the many hats he wore was as a fix-it man for the National Security Council. If for some reason a classified project was about to be compromised, he knew how to handle the local law enforcement, the local civilians, and especially the local press, in an effort to contain the damage—all while maintaining plausible deniability. He could only imagine this was the task awaiting him.

The copter came in from the east and landed on the B&B's front lawn. Shaw stepped out to find a small group of men waiting for him. Members of the Highway Patrol's antiterrorism unit, two Navy officers and a pair of local cops. Shaw quickly introduced himself as a DIA officer, his most convenient cover. It made little difference, though. The men all seemed to be in shock, especially the two local cops.

They climbed the cliff, and only then did Shaw see it: the hull of what was once a large ship, burning and twisted, not three hundred feet off the beach.

"What the hell happened here?" he roared.

One of the Navy officers told Shaw what he knew: how the ship was viciously attacked by a group of black helicopters no more than an hour ago, in broad daylight, and in full view of the local cops and about two dozen other witnesses.

Shaw couldn't believe it. He asked the man to explain it again. The officer complied, adding this further piece of information: Even though the ship had been torn up because of multiple weapons hits on its hull, what sank her was an immense explosion belowdecks. Something very volatile in the ship's hold had blown up as a result of the copters' attack.

Two Navy scuba divers were just emerging from the water below. They called up on a cell phone to the second Navy officer. Their report: Wrecked as it was, there was evidence the ship had been full of weapons. Not small stuff either. They'd found bits and pieces of rocket-propelled grenades, shoulder-launched SAMs, Katashuya rockets. Even a spent antiship rocket launcher.

Shaw was speechless. The cargo ship was obviously a gun runner, but not for the usual rifles and pistols. It had been carrying large and powerful weapons. High-grade *military* weapons, floating right off the coast of California. If the ship had ever unloaded and those weapons got into the wrong hands—it would have been chaos.

Shaw asked the CHP antiterror guys if the ship belonged to any known terrorist group. They answered no—at least not one that they knew about.

"We see small weapons coming in from South America all the time," one told Shaw. "But nothing like this. This was enough to equip an army."

Shaw felt his head start to hurt. Where did all this stuff come from? And where the hell was it all going?

"What can anyone else tell me about these helicopters?" he asked.

The local cops indicated that one of the B&B customers waiting up on the porch should join them.

"I can tell you about the helicopters," this man said to Shaw. "But I can also show you."

He held up a small digital camera.

"Take a look," he said.

Shaw studied the small readout screen, and sure enough, he could see a short video clip of the cargo ship being attacked. The footage began shaky and somewhat out of focus. At first it looked like something from a World War Two newsreel: the ship being rocked mercilessly by multiple explosions.

But then the camera zoomed out, and finally Shaw could actually see the attacking helicopters—and that's when he nearly lost it completely.

The copters were indeed black and unmarked.

But Shaw knew who they were.

X-Battalion . . .

The guys he'd just put out to pasture.

"Those bastards . . ." he growled under his breath. "What the hell were *they* doing here?"

PART TWO

CHAPTER 7

WEIR'S TEXTRON COPTER CIRCLED THE BRIAR PATCH
resort twice before setting down next to the flying-saucer-shaped meeting hall.

The flight back from Northeast Central had been uneventful, if unsettling. They'd gotten another eyeful of the simmering L.A. streets below—and things were only getting worse. The swarm of protesters had begun to march up from the beaches and toward downtown L.A. and Beverly Hills beyond. There were four vanguards of them and they really did look like ants on the move. Waiting behind their mile-and-a-half barricade along Santa Monica Boulevard was the LAPD. Equipped with gas masks, plastic shields and long wooden batons, they looked rock solid and unmovable. A disaster seemed unavoidable. Barring a miracle, the two opposing groups would collide in less than fifteen minutes.

A gaggle of security men were waiting on the helipad when Weir's Textron came in. Many more unseen eyes were watching as he stepped from the helicopter a few seconds later.

Two security men approached him. Weir already had his ID card out and was holding it at eye level. The security men were huge muscle-bound types who would have looked right at home playing goons in a James Bond movie. These people were either the A team from the Secret Service or members of the little known State Department Security unit. Whoever they were, they were obviously nervous.

They lingered over Weir's ID much longer than they had to. It was barely a plastic card with a bar code on it, but they studied it as if it had secrets hidden in code around its borders. They just didn't want to clear him in a snap—even though he'd been cleared to land, had been cleared to move about the site, and held a security clearance higher than ninety-nine percent of the people here. But this way they would at least appear to be doing their jobs.

They finally gave him a wave of clearance. Weir signaled his copter pilot, who shut down the aircraft's engines and settled back for a long wait. Then Weir headed for the saucer-shaped meeting hall.

Again, the UFO design was right out of the 1950s, an architectural style that was big in southern California back then and now. The structure itself was made entirely of glass, weirdly shaped panes, all with a ghostly emerald tint. Looking at it in the emerging sunshine reminded Weir of looking at something

through night-vision goggles. There was an odd spar-
kling quality to it.

He passed two more security men at the side doorway. They too studied his ID card with passionate indifference, making him stand in the broiling sun much
longer than he had to. Finally they let him through.

If anything, the interior of the meeting hall looked
even more futuristic. Weir had just assumed it would
contain nothing more than a large table and maybe a
few telephones. It did contain these things, but also one
wall featured a large-screen, at least 150-square-inch,
HDTV with hefty speakers hanging off its sides. There
were also banks of communications equipment lining
another glass wall, which especially lent itself to the
spaceship look.

The table itself was made of some black marble that
shone like glass. At each seat was a laptop, a wireless
phone, a crystal goblet and a bottle of mineral water. It
was silent inside the saucer room, except for the slight
whirring of the laptops and the banks of communications gear.

Weir's duties here were simple. Check the locks on the
doors, make sure they hadn't been tampered with, then
run an eavesdropping scan over all the communications
gear and around the room itself. This was all routine,
backup Agency stuff; just in case anything went wrong,
the Agency would be able to say they'd "stroked" the
building and, at least when they were in there, it was
clean.

It took him ten minutes to complete the bug sweep and check the meeting room's doorways. Everything came back as OK. The communications arrays were safe; there were no listening devices on or around the big screen TV. The pair of doors leading into the meeting room had not been tampered with.

Weir checked his watch. It was now 0900 hours. It had already been a busy day for him—and he was still behind schedule. But on the positive side, even though he would not talk to him unless there was an emergency, Denny Dana, his invisible go-to guy, would be arriving right about now.

Should anything go wrong, he knew Denny would have his back.

JUAN PINTO WAS THE GENERAL MANAGER OF THE Briar Patch Resort.

These were busy days for him. He'd only learned a week before that his facility would be the site of the WTO meeting. Though he'd catered to many celebrities and high government officials in the past—the membership at Briar Patch was ultra-exclusive—the thought of having the President of the United States along with nine other leaders of the world at Briar Patch was simply overwhelming.

So the last seven days had been a blur for him. The security issues he had to deal with were myriad. First, everyone on Pinto's management staff had to be checked out by the Secret Service. Forty-three people above the rank of assistant manager were investigated—nine of them had to be fired right away due to immigration issues. Of the thirty-four remaining, only six were actually selected to work the day of the event. Briar Patch would essentially be closed down for the twenty-four hours the WTO leaders were to be on the site. There was no need for the people connected to the golf course or the restaurant or the tennis courts to be on hand, as none of these facilities were to be used.

For him to be present, though, Pinto had a security check that went back to his childhood. Not only that, his entire family's background was checked, as well as his neighbors, and even his wife's personal trainer. The thoroughness of the security procedure was mind-boggling.

Pinto and the half-dozen remaining employees would be at the resort only in case something came up that the small army of security people and official handlers couldn't take care of. He and his crew would not meet the President, would not even see him, or any of the world leaders. They would be confined to a manager's office just behind the check-in desk, to be called on only if needed. Once on-site, they would not be allowed to leave or to converse with anyone outside the resort. Their meals would be brought to them. When it was time to sleep, each person would be assigned one of the resort's cheaper rooms—and locked in for the night.

Pinto would be the mother hen for all this—and only his best people would be staying with him.

Earlier this day, Pinto received a call, not from the Secret Service, but from the CIA. The spy agency planned to put an agent undercover at Briar Patch as a backup to the visible security force in place. As instructed, Pinto checked the veracity of the call with the Secret Service in charge of the security planning. Indeed, the Agency was going to plant a spy among Pinto's skeleton staff, just to get another set of eyes on the situation.

This agent, whose name was Denny, would take over the position as an assistant manager of Briar Patch for the next twenty-four hours. The CIA had deemed this prudent, and the Secret Service had concurred.

It was now 9:15 A.M. and Pinto was waiting at the resort's check-in area for the CIA plant to arrive. Having just been cleared through the main gate, he was expected momentarily. Pinto was on hand to greet him and show him to his quarters.

The operative walked through the front door one minute later. Pinto was instantly jealous of him: He had a full head of blond hair and a lithe muscular body. He looked like a Nordic god! The operative flashed his ID card, which, like many Pinto had seen in the past week, was simply a photo embedded in a bar code. Pinto greeted him with a fey handshake and formally welcomed him to the resort. Then he volunteered to show the operative to his room, to which the CIA man agreed.

Pinto led the way down the east wing corridor to the end of the hallway. The operative had been assigned Room 1, certainly not the cramped quarters that Pinto and his crew would be staying in when not on call.

As they walked down the hallway, two of Pinto's female employees went by, going the other way. Pinto had excellent hearing—and he clearly heard one woman whisper to the other: "Who is that? He's such a hunk."

They reached the operative's exclusive room; Pinto opened it with his pass key. The sunlight was flooding into the place as they walked in. Through the window and across the lawn, the saucer-shaped meeting hall was in full view.

The operative put his bag on the bed and nonchalantly opened it. Pinto put the man's clothes case across a nearby chair. By rote Pinto went into explaining the amenities of the room. The TV remote. The air conditioner. The Internet hookup. The operative thanked him, politely. Then he mentioned he didn't watch much TV.

As the man began to hang up his clothes, Pinto was able to eye the contents of his carrying case. It was not filled with suit coats or ties, but rather with electronic gear. And strangely enough, Pinto recognized some of it.

Before entering the world of hospitality, he had served in the U.S. Army as part of a logistics battalion. He'd cataloged, stamped, signed for and shipped out many frontline weapons to forward units, some of them being classified. What he saw in the man's clothes case was a Sperry YM-5 laser target designator.

This was a device commonly used by Special Forces personnel when on the ground in enemy territory. The operator would shine the laser on a target, such as a tank or an enemy building, so an aircraft, carrying a laser-guided smart bomb, would be able to home in on the laser beam, allowing it to release its weapon and have it follow the laser right down to its target. Pinto had seen hundreds of these devices before.

But for the life of him, he couldn't figure out why the CIA operative would have one here.

IT WAS EXACTLY NINE-THIRTY WHEN THE REAR GATES to Briar Patch opened.

With sirens blaring, nine long black limousines roared through the secluded entranceway, each followed by a heavily armored SUV. It took but ten seconds for the caravan to pass. Then the gates were closed again.

The procession didn't slow down as it proceeded along the golf course road and up toward the resort's parking lot. There, a large group of security personnel was waiting, Agent Gary Weir included.

The line of black limos and SUVs roared to a stop next to the saucer building. Bodyguards were suddenly moving everywhere. The sirens were turned off. Red carpets were rolled out. Weir yawned. The distinguished guests had arrived.

He watched with routine indifference as the back door of each limo opened on cue. Nine men in dark business suits stepped out. They were elderly white men, except for two Asians. No one with black skin, none with brown. And no women. A very exclusive club, to be sure.

Weir kept his distance, staying well behind the phalanx of security people who had joined the goons already standing at their stations. Just about everyone but he had an earphone stuck in his ear.

The dignitaries lined up and posed for pictures. Most seemed bored. A strange calm ensued as the only sounds were the official photographers' shutters going off and a chorus of swallows blithely singing away in the trees nearby.

Weir almost allowed himself to relax. His five-day horror story was finally approaching an end. All he had to do now was suffer through the rest of the welcoming ceremony, including the three-ring circus the administration insisted on putting on, and then wait for the tenth dignitary to arrive—the President of the United States, POTUS himself.

Once *he* was secure inside the meeting hall, Weir's day would be done.

So he closed his eyes for the first time in a long time and let the sun warm his face and the birds fill his ears. It seemed everyone was enjoying the silence for a moment as the photo session died down and the dignitaries made small talk among themselves. It was almost peaceful . . .

But the calm was suddenly broken by a loud electronic bleating. And just as suddenly, everyone—security people, dignitaries, chauffeurs—had turned from their conversations and were looking directly at Weir.

He didn't understand why at first. Then he realized what was happening: His cell phone was ringing.

He turned his back on the crowd and hastily answered the persistent phone. He had no idea who it could be.

"Who the hell is this?" he whispered furiously into the mouthpiece.

A very angry voice replied: "Major Jim Shaw . . ."

Weir was like . . . *what? Jim Shaw? The National Security Council's errand boy?* Weir and he had crossed paths over the years, but they didn't have much to do with each other. Why would he be calling?

"Sorry, Major—whatever it is, this is a really bad time," Weir told him in another urgent whisper.

"I don't give a crap!" Shaw exploded in reply. "Our mutual friends in Washington tell me that you reactivated Bobby Autry's outfit—*after* I had deactivated it!"

Weir rolled his eyes—everyone was still looking at him, he was sure. Is that what this was about? *XBat?* He'd almost forgotten about them.

"Rebooting Autry's crew was a necessary thing," Weir told Shaw hastily. He didn't need this shit from the NSC. Not now. Not ever.

But Shaw was furious, and *that* was coming through

loud and clear. He kept repeating his question, yelling at such a high decibel, Weir was sure the dignitaries could hear him.

"Calm down," Weir urged the Army officer. "X-Battalion just got a one-day reprieve. That's all. Nothing for your personnel office to get in a bunch about. They're just out at sea, looking for some wreckage. It's harmless."

There was a long silence on the other end of the phone. Weir could almost imagine the steam coming out of Shaw's ears.

"Let me inform you of something, Agent Weir," Shaw finally said, voice now low, speaking slowly but quivering with anger. "Your 'harmless' copter friends just *sank* a civilian freighter not three hundred feet off the coast, fifteen miles down from Laguna. They blew this thing to pieces, in front of a bunch of witnesses."

Weir's jaw fell open. *Did he just say XBat sank a ship? Down near Laguna?*

"Now let me ask you two things," Shaw went on, still on fire. "One—do you have any idea where X-Battalion is right now?"

Weir was speechless. But he only had one reply.

"No, I don't," he told Shaw truthfully. "No idea at all."

Shaw went on, still seething. "OK, number two: Do you know where the Alpha Point is in the Los Angeles area?"

The Alpha Point was an agreed upon location where

top intelligence people could meet in person under emergency circumstances. Anyone who was anyone in the spy business knew the Alpha Points in every major city by heart.

"Yes, I do," was Weir's reply.

"Then I want you there in ten minutes," Shaw spat back at him. "You and I have to have a nose-to-nose— right now. And you can consider that a direct order from the National Security Council."

A short pause, then Shaw added darkly: "And as you know, Agent Weir, the National Security Council acts only at the discretion of the President."

FIVE MINUTES LATER WEIR WAS BACK ABOARD HIS Textron, high above downtown Los Angeles.

The streets below looked even more crowded, more chaotic than just a short time before. The police presence had grown to awesome proportions. From the west hills to midtown there were police cars, SWAT vans, even armored personnel carriers. And thousands of additional cops in riot gear had appeared, not just on the streets but on the roofs of any building with a reasonably flat top, skyscrapers included.

But the number of demonstrators had swelled too. From the beaches to within just two blocks of the police line on Santa Monica, the long colorful mass looked like it was ready to burst at the seams. The whole thing seemed surreal—like a war that was just a few minutes away.

It took just five minutes for the Textron to reach its destination. Alberto started circling a flat piece of land in the hills, a splash of green grass amidst the brown flora. There were about a dozen people below. They were all walking dogs.

Canines and humans scattered as the pilot swooped in for a landing. Weir began to climb out. "Watch where you step," Alberto cautioned him.

Weir took a long look around, trying to get his senses. There was a light fog hanging over the high ground to his east, but now, as he stared up into it, it conveniently blew away. First he saw the silhouette of a steep hill, then the outline of a silver radio tower with dozens of cell phone antennae hanging off it.

Finally, he saw what he was looking for. The large, rather fragile looking sign. Nine big white letters, spelling out that one and only word: HOLLYWOOD.

This must be the place . . . he thought.

He trudged up the nearby path, and was instantly a ball of sweat. He was very uncomfortable leaving the resort, especially with the opening ceremonies not yet completed. But he had a window of time before the POTUS arrived. And again, if anything unexpected happened, Denny Dana would know what to do.

Still, he had only twenty-five minutes to spare—tops. So, whatever nightmare Shaw was going to lay on him about XBat, the natty major would have to be quick about it.

Weir climbed for another two minutes. His head was

lost in endless scenarios of how XBat could have fucked up to the point that it would attack a civilian ship. Finally he reached a clearing that brought him as close as possible to the hillside that served as home for the famous Hollywood sign.

Shaw was already here—and he was not smiling.

He started right in on Weir.

"What the hell were you thinking?" he roared at the CIA agent. "There are some people in Washington so pissed off at those XBat guys, if they find out they're flying again—we'll *all* be shoveling shit in Slovakia."

Weir wiped his mouth. It was bone dry.

"What's your clearance, Major?" he asked Shaw.

Shaw seemed genuinely offended. "I can guarantee it's much higher than yours, Agent Weir."

Weir was sure it was. But could he still let Shaw in on things he knew? He answered his own question with a simple: *Why not?* He wouldn't have much of a career left anyway. Not when his bosses got word of all this.

So he told Shaw the short version of everything. His overloaded work mission at Briar Patch. The cutter's mysterious disappearance. About how the Galaxy Net might be responsible.

"I asked XBat to look for wreckage," he told Shaw, calmly now. "We need to know if the Galaxy Net fucked up and sank that ship. If it did, there's the specter of 222 satellites up there, shooting deadly electronic rays down to Earth. How's that to ruin your day? So, XBat's mission was to help determine how the cutter went down. If we find out that the G-Net is fucked up, they'll have to shut the whole freaking thing down. And what will that be? A *trillion* dollars down the drain?"

Shaw looked like he needed a drink. So did Weir.

"Well, whatever you had them doing out there, they wound up sinking a goddamn ship in broad daylight," Shaw hissed. "Now, I was able to put a clamp on any press coverage about this for a couple hours, but it won't lie still for any longer than that. And I had to tell the local cops to put out an APB on Autry's crew—I had no choice. They're criminals at this point. Yet we'll *really* have a big pile of crap on our hands if Autry's guys are actually *arrested* by the California Highway Patrol. How do we explain the most top secret special ops group getting locked up by a SWAT team somewhere?"

Weir stepped back and thought a moment. Despite the ripping he'd just delivered, he could tell Shaw was not as mad as he should have been. In fact, he looked very worried instead.

"What the hell is *really* going on here?" Weir finally asked him.

Shaw brushed the dust from his jacket. He was still in his dress uniform.

"What's *your* clearance?" Shaw asked him, a rebuke.

Weir just shrugged. "Hey, you don't want to tell me, that's fine. Just one less thing to fuck with my head."

Shaw bit his lip. He had no choice but to share his intelligence with the CIA man, and they both knew it.

"That ship," he said slowly, "the one that XBat kiboshed? It wasn't a typical civilian ship. Not really. It was a cargo ship, a tramp, *filled* with lots of scary weapons."

Weir just stared back at him. "*What?*"

Shaw nodded darkly. "And I mean filled. To the top deck. Tons of the stuff. RPGs, antipersonnel rockets. Heavy machine guns. Even shoulder-launched SAMs and antiship missiles. Some Navy divers checked it out. They told me there was enough to outfit a small army. How it managed to get so close to California, or where the weapons were heading for, I shudder to think."

Weir felt like he'd been kicked in the stomach.

"Jesus Christ . . ." the CIA agent moaned. "There were two cargo ships right near the place where the cutter went down."

Shaw looked down at him. "You're joking."

Weir was shaking his head. "Jesus, I swear I never thought they were involved other than just being in the same part of the storm as the cutter. Our thinking was, whether it was a wave or a catastrophic explosion that killed the Coast Guard ship, then the two freighters eventually sank. But if they were armed, then . . ."

"Then they probably sank that cutter," Shaw said. "Something the G-Net never showed you, I take it?"

Weir just shook his head no. "But, while it might

have been the fuck-up of the century, if it was the same freighter that was out near that cutter, it's a good thing Autry's guys sent it to the bottom. Because that means all those weapons will not be on the loose."

Weir let out a breath of relief—but then felt the horror drain through him again. "But like I said, there were *two* freighters out there," he told Shaw. "And the remaining one might have weapons on it as well . . ."

Shaw nodded gravely. "They probably wouldn't be sinking Coast Guard ships if that wasn't the case. The problem is, we've got to find that second ship very quickly and quietly, without setting off every alarm in California. If for some reason we are wrong about this, we could start a panic that might become unmanageable."

Weir groaned in agreement. "And even if we turned it over to the Secret Service, or the LAPD, or anyone else," he said, "they would have to call in some special operators to look for it anyway, SEALs or somebody, and that will take hours to get ramped up, and that ship could be long gone by then. We don't have the time to take that chance. Not with all the crap that's happening at Briar Patch. If they have to cancel that dog and pony show now, who knows what the ramifications would be?"

Even as Weir was speaking, they both knew there was only one solution. No way could either one of them—or anyone else for that matter—arrange for another classified special ops team to get on-site in time to look for the second ship.

X-Battalion was the only unit in the area that could do the job.

If only they knew where they were.

CHAPTER 8

THEY WERE RUNNING OUT OF GAS.

It was now 9:35 A.M. and XBat had been in the air for almost two hours. But while each copter had the extended range capability to stay airborne for up to four hours, a long time for a rotary craft, they hadn't started this mission with full fuel tanks. They'd burned up nearly twenty percent of their gas while still playing their war games in the desert. There'd been no way, and nowhere, to get some more.

So, at the moment, the bottom line was this: While fuel consumption varied in the unit's trio of copter models, collectively speaking, XBat had about twelve more minutes of flying time left. After that they would have to start thinking quickly about finding a soft place to crash into.

But no one wanted to give up the hunt. *That* was the problem. The first freighter, the one with the dull yellow stack, was sitting at the bottom off Cliffside Beach, found and sunk after the unit began a determined search for the two rogue ships in the coastal waters south of the Port of L.A., the direction they were last seen heading. McCune had been the first to spot it in the thick fog and spray. Someone onboard foolishly fired a missle at him—this just as the rest of XBat had come on the scene. Not five minutes later, the ship was a flaming hulk. No quarter, no mercy. That's what happened when someone fucked with XBat. But they also knew the ship blew up not from their attack directly, but from a secondary explosion they'd set off belowdecks.

And that could only mean the ship had been carrying a lot of something that was very combustible.

BUT NOW IT WAS THIRTY MINUTES LATER AND THEY were down to nine minutes flying time. And still they hadn't found the second freighter.

They continued heading south, though, as their gas drained away. They were in full combat mode too, body and soul. No more chitchat, no more history lessons. Where before everyone had been wearing their military casuals on this, their last mission, now Autry and Zucker and everyone else in the unit was in their combat gear. Black battle suits, huge oversized battle helmets—called "Vaders," as in Darth Vader—fireproof boots and gloves, and flak jackets all round. As always, they were flying in radio silence. They were searching, with their eyes, with all their tracking gear. These were the guys who found the Doomsday Bomb in the lost mountains of North Korea, and an ICBM base hidden in the prehistoric jungles of Venezuela. They desperately wanted to find that second ship.

The unit had a formal pattern for ocean searches. Those copters that were more fuel efficient went farther out from shore. The mid-drivers—the Black Hawks— took the middle part of the search area. The gas guzzling Chinooks searched closest to the land—which was how McCune happened to spot the yellow-stacked ship.

But the team also had a safety procedure in place for these open water operations. It was called the QT Bingo. A confluence of time, speed and location—simply put, when the unit reached QT Bingo—they knew they would have to head for land, as their fuel reserves had hit rock bottom.

And if that were the case today, someone else would have to find the freighter. It would also mean a rather inglorious end to the X-Battalion.

They were less than a minute before QT Bingo now. Eight minutes of fuel would be needed to get back to shore and find a place to set down. It would be up to Autry to give the order to form up and head back for land. His last order, no doubt. But he desperately did not want it to end that way.

Thirty seconds to QT Bingo.

Autry was near frantic as they zoomed south, looking in every direction for the red-stacked ship, while

Zucker had his own eyes on the Black Hawk's FLIR system. This device projected out a couple miles, like a TV camera, looking for anything with heat. But they could see nothing.

Twenty seconds.

Autry threw on the surface radar—almost useless unless they were looking for something directly below them. Still, he scanned its readout screen, and saw only angry water.

Fifteen seconds.

Zucker pushed the telescoping effect on their FLIR, sending it out as far as it could go, several miles, weakened, but a last-second attempt to find something, anything. But still it came up empty.

Ten seconds.

Autry checked his watch and cursed. They were leaving the field of battle uneven—and the score would always be that way. When they wrote the history of XBat—not officially, but in their own hearts and minds—they would know in the end that the bad guys had gotten away with one. That they were up on them.

Autry knew that would be more than he could take.

Still, the time ticked away.

Five seconds to QT Bingo.

Five seconds to the end of XBat.

Four . . .

Three . . .

Two . . .

One . . .

Autry cued his chin mic, ready to give the Bingo order, when—suddenly—his flight computer started churning. Not with a radio call. They were still in radio silence. Rather, a photo was coming across his VDT screen.

The image scrolled itself down the page. It took just a few moments. When it was complete, Autry found himself looking at a very grainy, cloudy image of a rusty cargo ship—with an undeniably red stack.

The image was from Mungo.

He'd found the second ship.

"Damn," Autry breathed.

Zucker whooped; so did the guys in back.

But the momentary jubilation gave way to the cold hard facts. Mungo had indeed found the mystery ship about ten miles ahead. But the unit had also reached— actually *passed*—the QT Bingo point. They all had to dash inland before they wound up in the drink with empty fuel tanks.

In other words, XBat had found their last elusive quarry.

But at the absolute worst time.

CHAPTER 9

Briar Patch
10:00 A.M.

MANAGER JUAN PINTO WAS ASLEEP ON HIS FEET.

His knees were wobbly, he felt like he was catching a cold, and his stomach was turned up in knots. At this point, he wished he'd never heard of the President, and certainly wished he'd never voted for the man. The Chief Executive seemed to be absolutely ruining his life.

The Secret Service had lied to him; that was the reason he was feeling so sour at the moment. They had painted a picture of Pinto and his six trusted employees sitting in a single suite once the President had arrived, locked up tight, to be called on only if absolutely necessary. Pinto had brought his yarning books with him to read during what he was sure would be several hours of doing nothing.

Coffee? Danish? Could you get the director a Coke?

Can we get some towels for the prime minister of Japan? Why is the water in the bathrooms so cold? Why is the air conditioning making that squealing noise? The President will need ice for his water when he gets here. The President will need a new handkerchief. Do you have today's sports pages? Can you get them?

This is what the last few hours had been filled with—orders, for everything and anything. Always coming from someone on the President's advance staff, always with a mild threat dropped in at the end. No one had asked him nicely for any of this.

To accomplish most of these demands, Pinto had been forced to open up the resort's massive kitchen, a place that on a good day needed at least twelve people to work it properly. With only six employees, he was shorthanded right away. And it wasn't like he could just call a few people in. As it turned out, he and his chosen ones had been working their asses off ever since the whole bit of nonsense began.

Only adding to this trouble, Pinto knew things he usually did around the resort were going unattended at least by him. For instance, it was his job to visit the resort's electrical room once every two hours, just to check the various gauges, which told him that everything was working as it should. He hadn't been in the plant room in nearly a day. He was supposed to monitor the water pressure in the resort's own small firefighting system every six hours. The last time he checked the meter was the night before last.

He just had to assume someone else was doing these things now. Besides, he was too busy making sandwiches for all the President's men—and watching the kitchen's small TV as the unrest grew in the streets around the resort.

As there were more than eighty people on the President's advance staff, and they were all eating a lot, for free, at one point Pinto almost took the drastic step of asking his new assistant manager if he could pitch in and help in the kitchen. Could the spy slice Kaiser rolls? Could he unpack butter? Did he know how to make ice? Truth was, Pinto hadn't seen the CIA security man since delivering him to his room earlier.

By 10:00 A.M. Pinto and his people were already dog tired. It got so bad that he was filling water pitchers and coffee pots and delivering them to the administration's staff. That's how he happened to go by the CIA man's room. He'd just wheeled a cart carrying more water and coffee for the squad of presidential yes men that had holed themselves up in the resort's game room. Freely taking advantage of the TVs, the pool tables, and, Pinto suspected, the private bar, they barely nodded to him as he changed their coffee urns.

Walking back with an empty cart, Pinto passed by the suite where he'd left the undercover agent. It was strange—the man's door was still partially open. Pinto couldn't resist a peek inside, expecting to see the agent hooked up to some high-tech gear, listening in on everything anyone said anywhere in the resort.

But instead, looking through the crack in the door-way, Pinto saw that the man had not even unpacked his two big cases. In fact, he had barely moved from the last time he saw him.

Despite all the hubbub inside the resort, and the rising unrest in the streets around it, the man was lying on the bed, snoring peacefully away.

THE LITTLE TOWN WAS CALLED GRAPE RIVER.

It was located eighty miles south of Los Angeles, just off old Route 2, a half mile from the ocean. It sat in a small coastal valley, where, despite its name, only avocadoes and almonds were grown. Flat, open and isolated, Grape River had yet to come under the eye of southern California's ravenous developers.

There wasn't much here. A combination gas station and convenience store. A tiny post office. A farmer's co-op and an auto repair shop. The diner was only open until noon. The movie theater had closed in 1962.

There was a small airport nearby, however. The tiny facility was used only by the owners of the large almond groves surrounding the small town. It had just one air-strip, one hangar, a creaky control tower, and a 1,000-gallon aboveground tank holding aviation gas.

At the request of the half-dozen landowners who patronized the airfield, the tank was always full.

*   *   *

AUTRY'S COPTER WAS THE FIRST ONE TO PLOW IN.

His aircraft made a very undignified landing in a foot deep puddle of mud just off the airfield's cracked asphalt runway. How he'd managed to find this place was beyond explanation. Unlike further north, the storm had made landfall here, with rain squalls like waterfalls and the wind whipping around crazily. Flying in the vanguard of his unit, Autry had simply been looking for *any* piece of semiflat real estate to land their gas-starved copters.

Instead he'd come down on this airfield. A small one for sure, as there were exactly three planes tied up near the taxiway, shaking in the wind: two Piper Cubs and a very old, unusual Sperryman glass-cockpit biplane that looked like it hadn't flown in years. But there was also a small control tower here. And a hangar. And a fuel storage tank.

Even better, the place looked deserted.

One of the great things about XBat's copters was that they could run on just about any aviation fuel, just as long as it was combustible—and not a hundred years old. And landing unannounced at the tiny airport had raised hopes in Autry's heart. If they were able to get some fuel here and get airborne again, then maybe the chase for the second cargo ship wasn't over yet. Maybe XBat *would* have the last word.

It all depended on the quality of the fuel here. How good was it? Autry had to find out.

He and Zucker climbed out of their Black Hawk, carrying three gas cans between them. It was hard to see through the rain and fog how many of the other copters had landed nearby; a riot of microphone clicking as soon as they were down told them all eleven copters had at least made it down in one piece. But due to the harsh weather, it was impossible to determine just exactly where everyone was. The rain was so relentless and the clouds overhead so dark, it was almost like nighttime.

Undaunted, Autry and Zucker made their way through the muck and rain to the fuel tank. It was located next to the hangar; a roof sticking out of the side of the old Quonset-style aircraft barn protected the tank from the elements.

Soaking wet by the time they arrived, Autry first sniffed around the edge of the tank, then ran his ungloved fingers under the pour valve, feeling for a drop of whatever was inside the tank. Finally he felt something extra cool touch his fingertip. He immediately put it to his mouth and tasted it.

"I think it's AV-6," he told Zucker—the aviation fuel used mostly by civilian aircraft. It was lower quality than what XBat usually flew on—but it would certainly do.

The plan was to fill up the three cans and dump the contents into Autry's copter plus two others. These aircraft could then fly the short distance over to the tank, where they could be refueled easier with the twenty-foot pump hose. Then they'd fly off and another three would take their place. It seemed complicated, but XBat had trained for things like this—taking fuel on the run. Autry estimated the entire unit could be airborne within twenty minutes, barring any complications. He was almost giddy with the thought of getting back in the air and picking up the second freighter's trail again.

But that's when the complication showed up.

The old guy came out of nowhere. One moment Autry and Zucker were trying to solve the turn-on valve, the next this short, pudgy character with long gray hair and a scraggly beard was standing right next to the tank. He scared the crap out of both of them.

"Who are you guys?" he asked them simply, his voice a bit of a rasp.

The two pilots played genial. "We're with the FBI," Autry said. "We need to borrow some gas. Who are you?"

"My name is Kemp," came the reply. He was dressed like someone out of the 1840s. Old cowboy hat, plaid shirt, torn jeans, dirty boots, wearing a soaking wet duster. He was even chewing tobacco. "I'm the sheriff here."

"Well, we are authorized to do this, Sheriff," Autry said, nudging Zucker to get on with the gas appropriation process. "And we'll make sure this airport is compensated for whatever we take."

"Those are your helicopters out there?" Kemp asked them innocently. "How many you got? Ten? Eleven? Hard to see in this damn fog and rain."

"Should be eleven," Autry replied. "And I'm afraid we'll need gas for all of them."

Meanwhile Zucker had his gas can spout open and began to engage the tank's spicket.

"You boys have some ID?" Kemp asked them.

Autry and Zucker froze. ID? No one in XBat carried an ID. That was *verboten* in the special ops world.

"No—we don't have ID, Pops," Autry replied. "But we're in a hurry and—"

The next thing Autry knew, he was staring down the barrel of a very large, pearl-handled Colt 45.

"Who are you calling 'Pops'?" Kemp growled at him.

"Whoa, shit!" Autry cried out. "Take it easy, Pops!"

The gun got closer.

"*Stop calling me Pops!*" he roared. "I'm not even ten years older than you, you asshole."

As this was happening, just about the entire unit had emerged from the fog and walked up on the scene. It was a confusing one, to say the least. Autry and Zucker, literally caught red-handed stealing gas, the cowboy-type guy holding a hand cannon on them and spitting tobacky at the same time. It was like they'd all fallen out of an action movie—and found themselves in a Western instead.

"OK, everyone freeze," Autry told his men. "We definitely want to make sure no one gets hurt here . . ."

"Especially the old guy!" one of the troopers yelled, trying to be helpful.

The pistol was shoved farther toward Autry's nose.

"He's not that old!" Autry bellowed back, adding: "Now secure all weapons."

This meant "no one shoot the elderly cowboy." But it didn't make any difference. None of the XBat troopers had brought his personal firearm with him. All their weapons were back in the helicopters.

Autry tried again. "Sheriff Kemp—you can tell that we are a little unusual here, right? We're not typical soldiers. You have to believe me. We are on a special mission. For the CIA. For the FBI. You name it. I just can't really tell you who we are."

Kemp spit out another wad. "You don't have to tell me. I *already* know who you are."

The whole unit expressed surprise.

"Really?" Zucker challenged him. "How?"

Kemp pulled a long sheet of computer paper from underneath his coat. To the troopers' astonishment, it showed digital pictures of them attacking the first freighter.

Autry couldn't believe it. "Where did you get that?"

Kemp smiled—showing almost no teeth. "It's on the APB. That's 'All Points Bulletin.' Eleven helicopters. Everyone dressed in black. Special ops types. You guys are wanted criminals. And I've just captured you."

Zucker tried to laugh it off. They all did. "But we're not *those* guys," he tried to lie. "We're *another* special ops group. We're the good guys. They got us all flying because of this bullshit up in L.A."

Kemp laughed again. "Or you're the right guys," he said. "Want to know why I'm so sure?"

He kicked open the hangar door, which actually led into an office. He motioned Autry and others to look in. It was stacked with computers, modems, monitors—it looked like a tiny piece of Houston Mission Control. It was very elaborate, and unexpected.

"You guys are all over the Net," he told them. "You've got every cop down to the border looking for you. I just happen to be the lucky bastard you fell in on."

He raised his six shooter again.

"Now, on this APB it says 'hold for the Cliffside Police,'" he told them. "And that's exactly what I'm going to do."

He pulled back the hammer on the pistol again.

"Now all of you, get in the hangar, and put your hands over your head," he said. "Before I blow one of your asses off."

It took just a few seconds for the troopers to file into the hangar and line the far wall. Autry collapsed to the floor and tried to rub some sense into his very tired skull. This was all the team needed on this very screwed-up day. They'd found the second ship finally—only to run into Yosemite Sam?

But what could they do? Rushing the guy at this point would surely end in some kind of casualties—maybe fatal ones—to Sheriff Kemp and maybe one or two XBat guys. There was no way Autry was going to let that happen. Losing five guys for no good reason earlier was enough for him. And there was no way he was going to harm a fellow American citizen.

He looked around the darkened hangar. Their failed attempt to purloin some AV gas aside, he was surprised they'd all made it here alive. Or, at least, so he thought. *Was* everyone here? They seemed to be missing someone.

Autry took a quick head count and found the entire unit was on hand—except for Mungo and McCune.

He had not seen the last Killer Egg land—that would have been Mungo's aircraft. Nor had he seen McCune's Chinook bounce in, although the rest of his crew was here.

So, where were his two executive officers?

Autry stole a peak out the open hangar door. But still, he was having trouble making out any of the copters through the fog.

Then, out of the corner of his eye, he saw something strange: the small, very unusual Sperryman biplane was rolling down the airstrip's tiny runway, not a hundred feet away. How no one heard its engine start up or the noise of the plane taxiing, Autry didn't know. But as he watched, and completely unaware to Sheriff Kemp, the little plane went full throttle and jerked itself into the air in a very dangerous fashion.

It flew right by the hangar, so close that Autry could see into the cockpit. What he found was McCune and Mungo looking back out at him. Mungo even gave him a tense salute.

Autry couldn't believe it. While all the commotion was going on, this unlikely duo had somehow managed to assess the situation with Kemp and then steal an airplane.

But why?

And where were they going?

CHAPTER 10

THE SHIP WITH THE RED STACK HAD JUST ARRIVED off the beach at San Cuedo when the strange object appeared in the sky.

It was coming out of the northeast, and making a weird, screeching noise. Only a few people on the freighter's deck saw it at first. Most of the crew were down below, in the main hold, getting the ship's cargo ready for transfer.

This was a big moment for the ship's crew. It was important that the next thirty minutes go smoothly. They'd lost all contact with their sister ship, the one with the dull yellow stack, an hour ago. They were hoping it would appear out of the fog at any moment and join them in unloading. But if not, they had no choice but to proceed without it.

And things were coming together for them. The cargo was almost ready to unload. Their comrades onshore were signaling that they were in place as well. The storm, also close to land in this area, was even calming down a bit, which would make transferring the cargo to the small, isolated beach much easier.

But then this strange thing appeared in the sky.

It lost a little bit of its mysteriousness as it grew closer. It was obviously an airplane, a biplane in fact. But the bansheelike noise? That was the sound of a radial engine, being flown full-out, top speed, from 5,000 feet.

And coming directly at the ship.

"Is that thing crashing?" several people on the deck asked at once. *"Is it crashing into us?"*

They started shouting to those below. Something weird was happening up top. What should they do?

But the warning was a little too late. The strange airplane was already on them, its engine screaming, trailing a long line of black smoke behind. Panic washed over the ship. It didn't seem real somehow.

But just as it appeared the plane was going to slam into them, it suddenly pulled up and off to the right. The noise was incredible, almost unbearable; the smoke acrid and choking. The people on deck watched in shock as the plane roared by, narrowly missing them.

But there was something else going on here. Suddenly there were flashes of fire all around them. Sparks and hot metal were flying everywhere. Some of the crewmen were being literally cut off at the knees.

What was happening?

The plane took a tight turn and flew by them again. Only then was it clear that a man was hanging out of the open window of the strange plane. He had a machine gun and he was firing it at them.

The people aboard the ship couldn't believe it.

They were being attacked.

By a World War One biplane.

MUNGO HAD BEEN FLYING SINCE HE WAS EIGHT YEARS old.

He'd started out in crop dusters on his father's West Texas cotton ranch and worked his way up to flying training jets, during a hitch with the Air Reserves, and now to the most high-tech military copters in the world.

He'd never once become airsick.

Until now.

It was the way McCune was flying. Ever since they managed to escape from Grape River airfield—they'd arrived just in time to hear Kemp arresting the unit, but then slipped back into the fog—his fellow XO had been all over the sky. He knew when they stole the old airplane for the express purpose of going after the second freighter that it wasn't going to be any joyride. But the simple-looking Sperryman fighter was proving to be a real bitch to fly. And with their bad luck, it was only carrying half a tank of gas when they stole it.

Yet it had been enough to get them here, exactly five miles down the coast from where Mungo had last spotted the red-stacked ship, just before the unit went QT

Bingo. The bumpy ride had given him a very queasy stomach. But when McCune went into the gut-busting, eyeball-crunching suicide dive toward the ship—to "shake their pants," in McCune's words—Mungo nearly tossed his cookies. And now, still, McCune was gyrating all over the sky, flying way beyond the envelope for this sort of airplane—and expecting Mungo to fire his weapon out the window.

Yet this was exactly what Mungo was doing. And in truth, McCune was flying so close to the red-stacked ship that just about anywhere Mungo fired he was able to hit something.

The weapon was an M-16-12X—a high-tech, bulked-up cousin of the standard issue M-16. It was able to accept belt ammunition. It had laser aiming devices. It carried large incendiary shells that impacted on their targets at very high velocity. At the moment, those fiery shells were bouncing all over the port side of the ship.

Mungo's gunfire quickly found its way up to the control house—smashing the windows and causing a secondary explosion inside. Mungo also managed to sever the small forest of antennas sticking out of the snout of the red stack. This resulted in another fiery explosion.

McCune twisted the plane to the left, continuing into an 180-degree turn. In seconds they were streaking around the nose of the ship. Mungo kept on firing, even as he was trying to keep his stomach from turning itself inside out.

They went back around again, and for the first time

Mungo could pick out individuals on the deck. They were not shooting back at them; rather, the dozen or so faceless people were scrambling in every direction, trying to get out of the way of the wild barrage.

Another loop around the ship. The huge M-16 was chattering away, Mungo trying to shoot anything that might be combustible or high value. The ammunition belt seemed endless, his fire withering. And it was all very loud.

But in the end it was futile as well. Because as they rounded the stern of the ship a fourth time, the big gun abruptly ran out of ammunition.

This only deterred McCune for a few moments, though. In the time it took Mungo to pull the M-16 back into the cockpit, McCune was handing him his service revolver—a huge 12mm Beretta.

Mungo just looked at the gun—and finally got the idea. He stuck it back out the window and resumed blasting away. It was like firing a small cannon at the ship. But though he tried to keep up a continual if shaky barrage, the clip popped out before they were able to get halfway down the port side again. McCune quickly handed him another Beretta—he always carried two. When this ran out, Mungo took out his own pistol—a military issue Glock 9—and began firing again.

Five complete times around the ship and he succeeded in starting a number of fires, fucking up the ship's control house, cutting some if not most of the communications, and sawing a few of the crew in half.

But it was not enough. There was no way they'd inflicted so much damage that those on board would stop doing what ever they were doing. And that had been the whole point.

Even now, as McCune began a series of dry runs on the ship, Mungo could see a small fleet of rubber boats heading out from the nearby beach. Those on board the freighter finally realized the plane was out of ammo—and resumed getting their cargo ready for unloading.

McCune circled the ship a couple more times, but it was useless now. Not only were they out of ammo, they were also out of gas. He momentarily considered ramming the plane into the ship—and he probably would have if he was flying a heavier aircraft, and if Mungo wasn't onboard. But he knew the little plane would just bounce off the heavy freighter.

When they started taking scattered return gunfire from the vessel, it became clear there was no reason to hang around.

McCune cursed loudly, but then turned the plane away for good.

WITHIN MINUTES THERE WERE SEVERAL DOZEN small rubber boats pulled up to the side of the redstacked freighter. Two people were in each boat. Dressed all in black, each had a ski mask and a red kerchief covering his face.

Several larger boats were on hand too. Two were

yacht size, the others were commercial fishing boats. Their crews were dressed like the men in the rubber boats, all in black and faces covered with ski masks and kerchiefs.

The crew of the freighter began unloading wooden pallets over the side. The pallets were of all different sizes. Some were holding plain pine boxes, the size of coffins, each marked AIR FREIGHT. Other pallets had dozens of sports equipment bags strapped on them.

The people in the rubber rafts would snag the smaller wooden pallets, while the people in the larger boats went for the larger ones. As this was happening, dozens of men began climbing over the side. Dressed in black uniforms, as were their comrades, they used old-fashioned rope ladders to get down to the waiting fishing boats. The entire unloading procedure went surprising well. The seas remained calm, though, and that helped tremendously.

Once full, the small navy of rubber boats turned away from the ship and headed for shore. Several dozen similarly dressed individuals materialized out of the woods, waving them in. The rubber boats beached themselves, and now another unloading process began. The men on shore picked up the wooden boxes and spirited them into the underbrush. One of the yachts soon joined them at the water's edge and several large pallets holding the equipment bags were taken off it. These too were quickly hidden in the flora, the other boats close behind.

The entire operation took less than fifteen minutes. It was frenetic activity, but efficient. Within twenty minutes the beach was deserted, the rubber boats, the yachts, and the fishing boats were gone, and the cargo ship was heading out to sea at full speed.

Even the footprints in the sand had been brushed away.

THE SHIP'S BOOTY WAS TAKEN TO A CLEARING ABOUT a hundred yards in from the beach. It was surrounded by overhanging trees, making it impossible to see from the air. Three men had situated themselves here; they'd come ashore with the first of the wooden boxes.

Each box was now opened. There were 150 boxes in all. Each contained a rocket-propelled grenade launcher and four rockets. Each rocket carried a two-pound charge. Enough to penetrate the side of an Abrams tank.

The three men methodically went from box to box, removing the firing pins from the launchers. Then the boxes were sealed again. Nearly a hundred men had come ashore along with the heavy weapons; another seventy-five had been waiting in the bushes. Each box was now assigned two people. Picking up their boxes, these teams hurried out of the clearing and went farther down a sandy path, heading deeper into the woods.

Once the boxes were gone, the equipment bags were brought to the middle of the clearing. Each was opened and quickly checked. They each contained a fully loaded Stinger, an easy-to-operate, shoulder-fired antiaircraft missile. One man, in the right place, with one of these weapons, could shoot down an airliner, or a fighter jet. Or even a helicopter.

Once a bag was checked, it was given to its operator. He too quickly followed his comrades down the path.

The man assigning the weaponry was named Jerome. He was in charge of this operation—and now the hardest part of his job was done. Despite the bizarre aerial attack on the freighter, the weapons had made it to shore safely; so had the bulk of his men. As for the fate of the second cargo ship, Jerome feared it had been stopped or, even worse, sunk. No matter. He had enough guys and enough heavy weapons to do what he had to do.

The heavy weapons now on their way, Jerome pulled out a cell phone and punched in an eleven-digit number.

The other party answered immediately.

"Douglas? It's Jerome. We're having a beach party. Why don't you come on down? Our friend from Arizona will be here soon."

He hung up before any reply was possible and threw the cell phone deeper into the woods.

Then he followed his men down the sandy path.

A QUARTER MILE INLAND, THE WOODS MELTED AWAY and the desert began.

Waiting by the path that led to the beach were three tractor trailer trucks. They were indistinct, run-down and shabby, the sort of vehicle that hauled lettuce around southern California. Indeed, they'd been stolen from a produce farm near San Diego two months before.

The drivers were waiting nervously. Dressed in plain civilian clothes, they continually checked their watches and kept an eye on a large patch of high brush just off the road.

Soon a group of men emerged from the brush. They were wearing ski masks and kerchiefs. They waved to the drivers and the drivers waved back. Everything was set. They could proceed.

Working two at a time, the men in ski masks began carrying the pine boxes out of the woods and loading them onto the trucks, the sports equipment bags close behind. It was another quick if chaotic transfer; in minutes everything was packed aboard. Then the ski-masked people lined up in a loose military formation near the first truck.

Jerome came front and center and did a quick count; 192 bodies. Everyone was here. He gave them one last set of instructions, slightly muffled, as he was speaking through his ski mask. "You guys with the RPGs—just remember: Fire at anything you want once we get there, but make sure what you fire at is worth hitting. Maximum damage and maximum casualties—those are your orders. Those weapons are expensive. Don't waste them.

"Same with you Stinger guys. You see a target of opportunity flying overhead, line him up, and if you've got a shot, take it. Cops, TV copters, military—except for our friend—anyone with wings or a rotor is a target. But only take the shot if you got it squared up right. Those things cost ten times more than the RPGs, so be careful with them. Any questions?"

There were none.

On Jerome's signal, the men climbed into the back of the trucks, sealing the doors behind them. The three drivers started their engines and slowly drove away. The road was little more than a dirt path; it made its way through a particularly sparse piece of desert known as Soma Pits. It was a place populated only by scorpions and high tension towers.

If driving three tractor trailer trucks down a desert road like this seemed unusual, it wasn't. Not this road, not these kind of trucks.

This road was a major smuggling route for illegal immigrants sneaking across the border from Mexico. Though it would seem that someone—the INS, Homeland Security, *anyone*—would be watching the road, looking for illegals and busting the smugglers, the exact opposite was true.

Any smugglers traveling this route had already been "cleared." Meaning they had bought the needed protection to move unhindered by law enforcement or anyone else. The people employing Jerome and his men had simply bought this protection from a pair of local politicians. It had been one of the easier aspects of the overall operation.

It would take the trucks eighteen minutes to reach the end of this road. Once there, they would find a junction, which in turn would lead them to Route 52. A fifteen-minute ride to Route 14 would follow and then another ten minutes to get to the 82.

From there, they would be just twenty-two miles away from downtown Los Angeles.

CHAPTER 11

At Briar Patch

THE HUGE VIDEO SCREEN CAME TO LIFE WITH A FLASH.

The lights went down in Briar Patch's huge flying-saucer-shaped meeting hall and a visual faded up on the huge HDTV screen dominating one wall. It read: 1015 HOURS, LAUNCH ON SCHEDULE.

This dissolved into a shot of the open water. Clouds hung over the surface, but there was no rain, no sign of wind. Another visual appeared below this: 15 MILES OFF THE COAST OF NORTH SAN DIEGO. LIVE BROADCAST.

A moment later a submarine emerged from below the depths. It was an enormous vessel, nearly two football fields long, and weighed at least 20,000 tons. Unlike the black paint scheme of most U.S. subs, this one was painted an odd shade of blue. It seemed obvious that a vessel like this was rarely seen in public.

The seas were still choppy, though not so much as

to detract from the dark magnificence of the suddenly materialized underwater boat. It leveled itself on the surface and began moving at about 5 knots. A large red light attached to the sub's massive conning tower began spinning. Whistles and alarms commenced blaring.

Then, nothing . . . for about five seconds.

Suddenly the monstrous sub started shaking. The already choppy water around it began percolating as well. Then it seemed as if the air itself was shaking around the huge vessel.

A large door on the back of the sub suddenly blew away, a column of smoke and steam pouring out. In the next second, a huge missile roared out of the sub's oversized silo. This was not a typical SBM missile found on the Navy's other Trident submarines. This was twice the length, twice the girth, with a long sleek nose and booster rockets attached to its fold-out rear fins. More like something from a 1950s sci-fi movie than the twenty-first century, it was so big it looked like it could carry a substantial payload into orbit—satellites, weapons, even astronauts.

It rocketed away in a flash, a long-distance camera following it up like network coverage of the space shuttle. The booster rockets eventually fell away. A dramatic splash of flame a moment later showed the second stage separating. One more burst of fire and the missile finally passed out of sight.

The applause started slowly, hesitantly. The interior of Briar Patch's flying-saucer-shaped meeting hall, not unlike a spaceship itself, had been darkly silent while the images of the secret sub-launched missile played out on the huge HDTV screen. The invited guests, the dignitaries, and their staffs had stood, jaws agape as the strange spaceship rose into the heavens. They weren't quite sure what to think about it. Was it a weapon? A science vehicle? Both?

The visuals of the missile's launch alone had been amazing—almost *too* amazing. Whoever was responsible had somehow pulled off what had been essentially a multicamera shoot, including one with a very long range lens. Not an easy task out in the ocean. If some of the people in the meeting hall hadn't seen it for themselves, they might have suspected that the entire broadcast had been doctored somehow.

So, the applause was mixed with a few grumbles. Of them all, the Chinese representative looked the most uncomfortable.

The TV screen cleared, but only so another broadcast could take its place. This began, again, with a video shot of the open ocean. But this could not be the Pacific. The water was calm, the sky bright blue. It was more likely somewhere in the Atlantic.

Another visual appeared. It gave the time EST, and again, flashed the words "Live Broadcast."

A moment later a grayish object appeared in the far background. A second later it went right over the camera. Very high up, obviously flying very, very fast, it was an airplane of some weird design.

The camera turned abruptly, trying to catch the object as it rocketed away. The aircraft could just barely be seen passing over a very recognizable sight: the Statue of Liberty. This confirmed its location. The aircraft was presently over New York City.

A small clock appeared in the corner of the TV screen. The two words LIVE BROADCAST began blinking again.

The clock remained but the scene changed. Now the people in the hall were looking at Niagara Falls. Above the spray and mist of the titanic waterfall, the grayish aircraft appeared again. Once more it was very high, moving extremely fast, leaving a contrail that looked like a series of smoke rings on a rope.

Another visual appeared: CHICAGO SEARS TOWER. Again the plane could be seen streaking through the sky many miles above the huge skyscraper. The visual shifted again. Now it showed Mount Rushmore—and again the grayish aircraft appeared, still up in the stratosphere, still leaving the strange doughnut-holes contrail in its wake.

Another image filled the screen. It showed the Rocky Mountains—with the plane flying over them. Then the Grand Canyon, again the airplane and its weird exhaust trail, in full if hazy view.

At this point the conference members were asked to step outside. The clock in the corner had recorded less than twelve minutes.

The nine leaders walked back out onto the lawn next to the resort parking lot. One of the security people present had a pair of binoculars in one hand, a cell phone in the other. He shouted: "Here it comes!"

In the next instant the gray streak went right across the misty L.A. sky. Flying much lower, but just as fast, it was in view for a mere second. Then it disappeared into the clouds to the west.

Once more, the dignitaries were astonished. If what they had just seen was to be believed, this aircraft had crossed the United States in just twelve minutes.

But again, there was an undercurrent of whispers. Was this plane real? Or could the broadcast be a hoax? Had they just seen one ultraspeedy aircraft—or possibly several of them, simply flying over different if very recognizable parts of the United States?

It was hard to say.

But as it turned out, they didn't have much time to think about this as the administration's third ring of the circus was about to take place.

It arrived with the strangest noise of all. Not the roar of jet engines, not a rotary aircraft either. An aircraft that seemed a combination of the two had appeared over the resort. One moment the sky was empty. The next, this strange aircraft was just there. It most closely resembled an OS-22 Osprey, the VTOL aircraft that acted both as a cargo plane and a helicopter. But this thing was no Osprey. It was much bigger and also very streamlined. It didn't have huge movable propellers stuck on the end of its wings like the Osprey. This aircraft had jets, or rockets, or something, hanging off these appendages. They were responsible for making the odd, almost burping sound.

The people on the ground had never seen anything like it. It went into a perfect hover above the spot where the dignitaries had gathered. The strange aircraft directed a bright white light on the resort parking lot. Then it began descending.

It came down smoothly, if a little bit too fast. Bouncing once on first contact with the asphalt, it stayed down for good the second time. A minute went by, then two. Finally, the side door opened and a lone figure stepped out. He was dressed in a flight suit, all white, with a large fighter pilot helmet covering his head and obscuring his face.

No sooner had he cleared the wing when the strange burping noise appeared once again. The aircraft rose straight up, to about five hundred feet. Then, with its wings pointed forward again, it exited the area at tremendous speed, leaving the passenger alone on the asphalt.

Security men ran forward. In seconds the man in the flight suit was surrounded by armed guards, each with an earphone and a small concealed microphone in his hand.

The person in the fighter pilot suit took off his helmet and ran his hand through his hair. A mild gasp went through those assembled.

It was the President of the United States.

This dramatic arrival—he would later claim he flew

the strange machine there himself —was the final piece of the administration's dog and pony show. And if the purpose had been to shock and awe the visiting dignitaries, then at least one thing had gone right today. The grand entrance had made a huge, if somewhat suspicious, impression on most of them. Others though—the French, the Germans, and the Chinese—were bristling with displeasure.

A microphone had been hastily set up on the asphalt. The Chief Executive, known to his Secret Service detail as "POTUS," strolled over to it and tapped it once to make sure it was on.

Then he said: "Gentlemen—welcome to Beverly Hills. Now let's get this meeting started."

IT TOOK JUST A MINUTE FOR THE DIGNITARIES TO file back into the meeting hall.

The security people repositioned themselves as well, taking up stations at all the doors leading in and out of the saucer-shaped structure. This left only Gary Weir standing out on the asphalt, not relaxed but at least a bit relieved.

The sub-launched orbital missile had gone off without a hitch, as had the breathtaking Aurora flyover. The foreign members of the WTO were left suitably impressed, if not exactly for the reasons the administration had hoped.

At least all that was over, Weir thought. The POTUS

was in the house—literally—and for the most part that meant he was someone else's problem now.

But Weir's day was not over—not by a long shot. He still had the other major fuck-up to fix: XBat and the two mysterious cargo ships.

He and Shaw had left their uncomfortable meeting deciding only one thing: that Shaw would start the search for XBat while Weir returned on-site to cover the President's arrival at the WTO meeting. But now that his duty here was over, Weir had to join the hunt for the rogue X-Battalion —a difficult thing to do for a unit so secret they never did anything that wasn't in the shadows and under total radio silence.

The plan now was for Weir to reconnect with Shaw, via the Army officer's private cell phone number, and together they would try to divine the whereabouts of XBat and attempt to rein them in.

But before he could dial Shaw's number on his phone, the phone began ringing.

It was not Shaw, though.

It was the clerk at the crap hotel in Northeast Central.

He identified himself through a code word: *Weatherman*. Then he spoke another code word that ran a chill right through Weir: *Rainstorm*.

This word meant only one thing: *Get over here right away*.

*   *   *

INSIDE A MINUTE, WEIR'S TEXTRON COPTER WAS back in the air and once again roaring over the heart of L.A.

As it turned out, the sky above the city was a traffic jam of LAPD copters, Highway Patrol copters, government copters, and many, many TV news copters. The Textron barged its way right through this aerial crowd, though, the other aircraft making way for the high-tech, all-black aircraft as it headed straight for the slum known as Northeast Central.

It took just five minutes to fly there. The niceties of covert ops aside, Weir's pilot set the Textron down right in the middle of the seedy motel's parking lot.

The clerk was waiting for them when they arrived. Standing at the top of the rusty staircase, his hands and shirt were smeared with blood. He was in tears.

"I don't know what happened," were his first words to Weir as the CIA agent rushed up the stairs. "I didn't hear anyone come in. Didn't hear anyone on the balcony. Didn't see anyone on the security camera."

Weir brushed past him and stepped into the decrepit motel room. A lifeless form was sprawled in the doorway of the unit's filthy bathroom. It was Denny Dana. He was dead. His neck had been broken by way of a garrote, and he'd been stabbed in his throat.

Weir walked over to the body. Dana still had a brochure for Cape Cod clutched in his hands.

Weir reached down and touched the man's arm. It felt ice cold. Dana had been dead for at least an hour. That meant whoever killed him had done so shortly after Weir's visit earlier that morning.

Weir nearly lost it right then and there. He was a mess before this had happened. Deprived of sleep, sick on coffee and speed, stressed out, flipped out—and now this: his friend, horribly murdered.

He angrily turned on the clerk. *"How the fuck did this happen?"* he bellowed at him. "What the fuck are we paying you for?"

The guy was still in tears. He was obviously in shock too.

"I told you," he insisted. "I didn't hear a thing. There's nothing on the video."

Weir turned Dana onto his back. The garrote had been made not of rope but of shoelaces, impossible to lift a fingerprint from. There was very little postmortem bruising, indicating a quick, clean twist of the neck. The stab wound in the neck almost seemed an afterthought.

Weir felt his own body go cold. He checked the bathroom's boarded-up window. There was a small pile of splinters and dirt along the bottom of the frame. The piece of plywood covering the window had been moved recently. Weir gave the plywood a slight tap. It fell off, dropping into the side alley below. Only one nail had been holding it on.

The pieces of the puzzle started to fall together. Someone had climbed up from the alley, come in through the bathroom window, and caught Dana when his back was turned. The video camera did not look directly into the bathroom. The intruder must have known this.

A quick entry. A quick murder. A quick escape.

This was someone who knew what they were doing. An expert . . .

Weir returned to the room and did a quick scan of its contents. Dana's pistol was still under the pillow. It had not been moved since Weir's visit. His money, clothes, and even his ID badge were still in evidence. None of them had been touched.

Two things were gone however: Dana's cell phone and the bottle of hair dye.

That's when it dawned on Weir what a huge blunder he'd just made.

He pulled out his own cell phone and sent a text message, again with a single word: *Quarterback.*

This too was an emergency code word.

To his horror, he received a one-word reply: *Fullback.*

This was the agreed upon code word that Dana was supposed to send to him to let him know all was well inside Briar Patch.

"Damn," Weir whispered.

If Dana was here, dead—then who was at the resort?

CHAPTER 12

Adams Air Force Base
Arizona

THE FOUR A-10 THUNDERBOLTS TOOK OFF, TWO AT A
time, leaving a trail of dirty exhaust in their wake. They
rose to 5,000 feet and turned north, the dry morning air
giving their engines a high-pitched sound.

The four attack planes belonged to the Arizona Air
National Guard. This was a training mission, one of
four the Guard pilots practiced per month. Today was a
typical—and routine—air-to-ground gunnery exercise.

In many ways the A-10 was a gun with two jet
engines attached. It carried within its fuselage a large
rotary cannon called GAU-8. This was a weapon so
fearsome—the shells were nearly a foot long—it could
reduce an enemy battle tank to cinders in seconds.

Each A-10 was also carrying a pair of laser-sighted
missiles known as Hellfires. These weapons were also

designed to take out tanks—as well as troop trucks, mobile guns, and artillery. The missile carried a small but powerful warhead with a laser tracker attached.

Once launched from the aircraft, the tracker could guide the Hellfire down to any target that was laser-illuminated. In other words, if an accomplice on the ground was able to shine a laser marker on a target, the Hellfire would detect the marker, and home right in on it. The resulting explosion could demolish an entire building.

Within two minutes of take-off the four A-10s were within sight of their target range. On this five-square-mile piece of restricted desert area, various targets had been set up for the A-10s to shoot at. Old tanks, old jeeps, cement structures and things that mimicked enemy bunkers were scattered everywhere. The plan called for each A-10 to launch a single Hellfire, then take two strafing runs with their big aerial gun. In all, the exercise would take just five minutes.

At one minute out from the range, the A-10s' flight leader ordered the rest of the Thunderbolt pilots to update their computers. This was a procedure to make sure every plane, and every pilot, was on the same page. It was a matter of pushing a few buttons and allowing the computer to clear its head. Then, again by proce-dure, each pilot was to report back to the flight leader that all was well.

The second plane in the flight did this almost im-mediately. His computer having been flushed, he would be the first plane over the target range. Plane three also checked in, its pilot reporting everything was green.

The flight leader then called the pilot of the fourth plane. But there was no reply.

The flight leader tried again. They were only seconds from reaching the gunnery range; their time over it would be limited. This was not an occasion to dawdle. But the flight leader's second radio message also went unanswered.

When a third attempt also failed, the flight leader turned his jet so he could look behind him.

The fourth A-10 was gone.

MORE THAN A DOZEN PEOPLE TRIED TO MAKE CON-tact with the fourth A-10 over the next few minutes.

The flight leader never stopped calling his wayward pilot, as did the other two pilots in their flight. But the control tower at Adams AFB was also trying to contact him, as were air traffic controllers at the Phoenix airport and six smaller private airports in southwest Arizona. But even though Adams AFB communications could tell that both radios aboard the A-10 were working, for some reason the pilot was unable or unwilling to acknowledge the calls.

The A-10 was spotted five minutes later by a local commuter flight. The commuter pilot reported that the plane was circling Jackson Mountain, a hundred miles from the California border. It seemed as soon as the pilot of the A-10 saw the commuter flight, though, it changed its course and shot off at high speed to the north.

Not a minute later, the A-10 was picked up on radar at a small airport nearby. It was detected flying very low at times, then zooming up to 20,000 feet, before plunging just below radar again.

At just about the same time, the ghost plane was spotted by a former pilot hiking in the hills more than fifty miles from the target range. He saw the A-10 had punched through a sucker hole, a small space in the overcast. He watched as the plane carried out some bizarre but obviously controlled maneuvers: screaming climbs, screeching dives, gut-wrenching, multi-g turns. Twice the A-10 almost flew right into one of the nearby mountains.

The ex-pilot knew this was not right, especially since the A-10 was obviously carrying weapons. He called the nearest air base, which was Luke Air Force Base, near the Nevada border, and began a conversation with the tower. The base's security officer was summoned, and at his request the ex-pilot provided a running dialogue of what he was seeing.

The A-10's antics continued for the next two minutes. Seemingly intent on ripping itself to pieces, the 'Bolt's pilot was stressing his wings and pushing his dive pull-out capabilities way beyond the envelope of the stout attack plane, only to climb back up to 20,000 feet and try it again. As this was happening, the tower at Luke

AFB tried contacting the pilot again. They told him he was in sight of a former pilot and that if there was a mechanical or a health problem causing his bizarre behavior he should straighten out if possible and wag his wings, letting the observer know that he understood.

Incredibly, the A-10 did straighten out—for about two seconds. Then it turned violently on its wing again and flew right at the hiker's position. The ex-pilot continued watching it as it roared over his head and turned southwest, letting Luke AFB know when he finally lost sight of it.

"Can you tell where he's going?" the tower queried the ex-pilot.

"If you ask me," the man replied, "I'd say he's heading right for Los Angeles . . ."

CHAPTER 13

THE BATTLE OF L.A. BEGAN AT PRECISELY 10:35 A.M.

That was the moment a swarm of anti-WTO protesters hit the LAPD barricades along Santa Monica
Boulevard. They came in force, swinging baseball bats
and pieces of rebar. The sheer ferocity of the protesters'
charge startled the police. They'd been expecting nothing more than some rock and bottle throwing at first,
because, according to their vaunted riot training, that's
how all anti-WTO protests began.

The sudden onslaught caused the police line to bend
near the corner of Santa Monica and Sunset, one of its
weakest points. The protesters pressed forward, even as
the cops were trying to beat them back with their riot
batons. Suddenly, tear gas filled the area—but it had not
been activated by the police. The protesters had brought
their own. And as no one had ordered the cops to put
on their gas masks yet, they were caught by surprise a

second time. The protesters surged ahead again and the police line bent even further.

An LAPD lieutenant named Johnny Gomez was in charge of this part of the police line. He had 250 cops under his direct command, all of them trained in riot tactics and crowd control, all of them stretched twenty feet in front of him, suddenly battling furiously with the onrushing demonstrators. This was not good. Gomez and his men had been preparing for this day for weeks, but again, that training had been based on what happened at past anti-WTO demonstrations: rocks, bottles, maybe a Molotov Cocktail or two, with moderate property damage to nearby stores, and a constant ripple up and down the police line, but never any concerted attempts to break through.

What Gomez was looking at now—a concentrated, almost pinpoint assault on a small part of the overall line—hadn't been covered in the training.

"This isn't how it's supposed to go!" he cried as his men buckled further.

That's when a second, even more concentrated wave of protesters hit the police line. Gomez saw them coming. There were maybe a hundred or so, again many armed with baseball bats and rebar. But to his horror, Gomez saw some of the demonstrators carrying something else: AK-47 assault rifles.

Before he could do or say anything, these dozen or so armed protesters began firing point-blank into the line of police, many of whom were still struggling to get their gas masks on. As there had never been a single instance of gunfire at an anti-WTO protest before, for the third time in less a minute the L.A. cops had been caught disastrously off-balance.

Suddenly, bullets were flying everywhere. Bodies were falling, screams permeated the air. To his astonishment, Gomez's men began to turn and run—and just as quickly, he was running with them. The police line on Sunset had broken.

Falling back in disarray, Gomez tried to form another line near the corner of Pueblo and Lancaster Boulevard. Only about fifty of his men stood with him, though— the rest kept right on running. Neither Gomez nor any of his men were carrying real weapons; they were forbidden in riot duty, as there was always the fear that an unarmed protester, or a bystander would get shot by accident. But never did the LAPD think they'd be facing *armed* protesters. Having no other choice, the few dozen cops in this shaky second line began firing tear gas canisters directly into the oncoming wave of demonstrators. But the protesters were prepared for this as well, and many were already wearing gas masks. They simply hurled the smoking canisters back at the police and then charged them again under the smoke. More gunfire filled the air. More cops went down. Gomez's men broke again.

He also turned to run, the chaos filling his ears, panic rising in his chest—but then he realized he couldn't move. He looked down at his feet, as if they'd become stuck in cement, and saw that he was bleeding heavily from his navel on down.

He was stunned—for about two seconds. Then the shock and pain hit him, both at once. It was so violent his feet were knocked out under him. He crashed hard, face first to the asphalt. Only then did he realize he'd been shot.

He managed to look up and see the last of his men streaking by him as if in fast motion. Some were even jumping over him, so intent were they at escaping with their lives. The wave of demonstrators was right behind them. Some ran right over Gomez, splitting his stomach open even further. Then, from the corner of his eye, he saw one protester stop above him. The man had both a ski mask on and a red kerchief across the bottom part of his face.

Even as life was running out of him, Gomez wondered: Why would this guy be wearing *both* a ski mask and a kerchief?

That's when he saw the man's assault rifle.

"Please, don't," Gomez tried to plead with him. "I've got two young kids . . ."

But the man just laughed through his mask. Then, very casually, he put his gun barrel against Gomez's forehead and pulled the trigger.

THE BREAKTHROUGH AT SUNSET CAUSED THE REST of the police line along Santa Monica to go limp. As more and more demonstrators poured through the gap at Sunset, police commanders rushed reinforcements to seal the hole. But this just further diluted the overall line. A second charge from the demonstrators hit the police position one block up from Pico, again at a place where the LAPD was at its weakest. There was gunfire here as well, all of it coming from the protesters' side. In seconds another breach was formed.

Now, like a dike broken in two places, dual streams of demonstrators flowed through the police line. Crossing over Olympic Avenue, they began rampaging their way up toward Bradley Street, smashing windows, starting fires and overturning cars. Any policeman or civilian they came to was either shot or beat to a pulp. Most bizarre, people working in the skyscrapers surrounding the trouble zone were at their windows, looking down on the chaos and only now realizing they might be trapped by it.

When a third wave of protesters hit Santa Monica at Melrose, the entire police line collapsed for good. There was even more gunfire here, and sensing victory in the air, the protesters fell upon the police without mercy. What should have been a slow, but orderly retreat by the cops quickly turned into a rout. Some simply ran, others jumped into police vehicles and roared away, the members of the press right behind them.

It seemed unthinkable, but that's what happened. At the first indication that they were going to be overwhelmed, the LAPD broke ranks and ran, leaving thousands of citizens behind to fend for themselves.

WATCHING ALL THIS FROM ABOVE WAS GARY WEIR.
His Textron copter had been rushing back to Briar Patch from the seedy motel when the nasty little war finally broke out below.

Just twenty minutes before, when he'd flown over the city in his dash to Northeast Central, it had appeared that the LAPD held a firm upper hand in the situation. He'd seen thousands of cops decked out in heavy riot gear that looked more like military special ops outfits. With their battle helmets, plastic shields, armored cars and water cannons, the cops below had looked like an urban army of the future.

Now they were an army in retreat.

Weir was in a great rush—he had to get back to the WTO meeting and tell someone, *anyone,* that his inside guy was not who he seemed to be. That someone had murdered the real Denny Dana and had taken his place, with plans to do God knew what. As it was, he was speed-dialing every Secret Service number he had for the Briar Patch, but they were all busy. A possible sign of trouble . . .

But what was happening on the streets below was *also* suddenly important. The whole basis of the security plan at Briar Patch was that the LAPD would be able to contain the protesters to certain areas of downtown and ensure they got nowhere near the exclusive Beverly Hills resort. In fact, in the planning documents Weir had seen, the LAPD had boasted the protesters wouldn't get within a mile of Briar Patch. From what Weir could see now, though, flying five hundred feet above the city, some of the protesters were already moving en masse along I-405, past West Hollywood, and heading directly toward Beverly Hills. And Weir couldn't see a cop within twenty blocks of them.

This was not good. It was obvious the LAPD had broken down very quickly and that the situation in all of Los Angeles was now bordering on chaos. Sick with the image of Denny Dana's bloody body burned onto his retinas, Weir was wondering if what he was seeing below was a coincidence or not. The LAPD instantly dissolving away; a mole inside Briar Patch itself; the two weapons ships being chased by XBat.

Something clicked in his brain. Maybe this wasn't just a demonstration gone wild here.

Maybe this was a coordinated attack . . .

He slapped his pilot Alberto on the shoulder, his way of telling him to open it up, that they had to get back to Briar Patch as quickly as possible. But no sooner had Alberto assured him they were going all out when the Textron's flight computer lit up like a Christmas tree. A loud alarm began blaring.

"What the hell is that?" Weir cried.

Alberto pointed to his control panel. A touch screen was blinking madly: AIR DEFENSE SUITE—WEAPON LOCK-

ON. It took about two seconds for Weir to realize what this meant.

Someone had fired a missile at them.

Alberto went into automatic mode, his hands and eyes moving everywhere. One hand wrapped around the collective control, the other pushed a defensive measures panel on his flight board. The copter immediately went up on its tail and then looped over, all in one violent motion. The engines screamed in protest—this was *not* the way to fly a helicopter. But the guy doing the flying was not a typical helicopter pilot.

At the same time, the Textron began spitting out flares. Weir knew there were two ways to fool a SAM—evasive, if gut-wrenching maneuvers, and hot flares. If the zigzagging didn't throw off the missile's heat-seeking nose cone, the high temperature of the flares would.

All this happened in a matter of microseconds. Used to such aerobatic rodeo moves, Alberto had instinctively held on as soon as he heard the defensive suite start barking. Weir, not as used to this sort of thing, didn't. He slammed into the cockpit glass as soon as the pilot started his evasion procedure.

From this point of view, Weir was first looking straight up into the deep blue sky—and then straight down at the troubled streets below. The violent maneuver had happened so fast, his already queasy stomach didn't even give him the chance to puke.

"It's a Stinger!" Alberto yelled. "Right side, coming up fast! Here is it—right now!"

The missile went by their nose an instant later. Alberto didn't stop to admire it. He continued the evasive turn, banking at a very sharp angle and heading back toward the line of flares he'd shot out. This put the nose of the copter pointing in the direction from where the missile had come. At the moment, it was the safest place to be.

Only then did it dawn on both men what had just happened. *Someone on the ground had fired a missile at them*—something that was an almost daily occurrence in Iraq or Afghanistan. But it had just happened over Los Angeles.

"That was a first," Weir said aloud.

And it was at that moment, heart still pumping from the evasive maneuver, as he wondered how the implications of what had just happened would play out, that he looked back out the cockpit window.

That's when he saw a second SAM coming at them. And this time the defensive suite never had a chance to go off.

The missile hit the rear end of the Textron a moment later, blowing the helicopter in two.

CHAPTER 14

MAJOR JIM SHAW HADN'T STOPPED MOVING.

Since leaving the Hollywood sign, since sending Weir back to Briar Patch, he'd been in constant motion. All thoughts of getting back to Washington anytime today were long gone. But that didn't matter. They had the makings of a huge political crisis here—one that would land squarely on top of the huge security crisis already playing out in downtown Los Angeles. A foreign ship filled with state of the art military weapons had been sunk in U.S. waters by secret U.S. forces not far down the coast from where the President was hosting the nine most powerful men in the world. And still with the possibility that a second ship was out there somewhere, filled with weapons as well.

It didn't get any worse than this. And Shaw knew he had to do something about it. And that something was to find XBat.

In his twenty-five years working the DIA side of the

National Security Council, he'd been in these types of situations before. Covering up outrageous events was part of his job. None had been as grand as this one, though, and so far they'd all happened overseas. But in containing them, he'd always followed a set list of rules, a formalized procedure. Running this particular drill had always worked in the past. He just hoped it would work now.

That's why he was waiting in line at the Bank of America on the corner of Wilshire and Hollywood Boulevard at the moment. He had a credit card in his hand that held nothing more than a gold magnetic stripe and a bar code. When he reached the teller's window, he simply gave her the card and told her he'd like to make a manual debit withdrawal. In effect, she swiped his card—and discovered a bank account that contained several million dollars.

"I'll only need twenty thousand," he told her calmly. "All thousands, if you can."

The teller checked it with her manager, who recognized the card's security code as, on one hand, belonging to the U.S. Department of Agriculture, but with a second security scan showing up as the U.S. Army. The manager released the funds.

Shaw then hurried across Wilshire to Vine, to another bank, this one the Bank of Southern California. He produced another unmarked credit card, and the teller handed him a key. It unlocked a safe deposit box in the bank's vault, which held a massive Magnum 500 pistol and several boxes of ammunition. These drop sites were always available for intelligence operatives in any big city. Like Shaw, you just had to be high enough on the food chain to know where to look.

Armed now with both money and a weapon, he headed for an even more unlikely place: the local library.

His driver for all this running around was a uniformed member of the Los Angeles Sheriff's Department Emergency Services Squad, L.A.'s home-grown Homeland Security people. Given to Shaw at his request after his visit to Cliffside, the young cop was brilliant in getting him where he had to go, all the while avoiding the chaos and urban warfare that had broken out just twenty blocks away in downtown Los Angeles.

The trip to the library was the weirdest stop of all. The first one they came to was in a run-down multiethnic district. The librarians profiled them immediately as being government agents, snooping around, Patriot Act and all that crap. Shaw was polite as possible. He needed the use of a computer, one that had at least 100K of RAM.

The library had one such machine in its research room. The librarian wordlessly set up the machine so Shaw could get on the Internet. As the Sheriff's Department driver stood guard, Shaw began banging his way through dozens of Web sites that served as firewalls set in place by myriad U.S. intelligence agencies. Shaw knew all the code sequences by heart and soon accessed the site he needed.

Once he'd broken through the last encryption barrier, the sequence he punched-in was simple: *GalaxyNet. com*

When he was in, Shaw instructed the monstrous satellite system to show him views of the southern California coast line two hours earlier. He fine-tuned the request several times until he was looking at a streaming video of the first cargo ship being attacked off the coast near the small town of Cliffside.

Though mirroring what he'd seen earlier in the witnesses' home video, Shaw was in awe as he watched the eleven XBat copters pounce mercilessly on the cargo ship, firing at it nonstop until it blew itself out of the water. It was like watching an action movie with supreme f/x. The destruction of the freighter had been so quick and so complete, it was amazing any wreckage had been left at all.

He then ordered the Galaxy Net to follow the helicopters as best as it could once they'd left the scene, a chore even for the trillion-billion-dollar spy system. It continued its search down the California coastline, showing Shaw a collage of vistas of stormy sea conditions and rain squalls, with only fleeting glimpses of two or three of the ghostly high-tech XBat copters— they always seemed to be flying tantalizingly close to the edge of the frame.

But just forty seconds into this, Shaw at last saw something else. Another cargo ship. This one with a bright red stack. It was sailing in choppy seas farther down the coast, trying to stay hidden in the fog banks enveloping the waters surrounding the channel islands. Again, there were only teasing images of this phantom ship, but there was no doubt that it was real, and that XBat was chasing it.

There was no happy ending here, though. Just as the cargo ship slipped in and out of the Galaxy Net's own version of reality, so did the pursuing helicopters—until, one by one, they began disappearing from the montages, until only the ship remained, still moving very fast, through the foggy waters near Catalina.

It was clear to Shaw what had happened: XBat had been on the tail of the second ship as well—until they ran out of gas. This had to mean they all headed back to shore and set down somewhere. But where? There were so many places they could go, and knowing the XBat unit, they would have probably hidden away by now, as per their talents, camouflaging themselves in such detail that even the Galaxy Net would not be able to see them.

Shaw sank into his seat. The second weapons ship had been lucky. It avoided the pounding its sister ship had received only because the capters had run out of gas. The ship had been allowed to continue on its dastardly mission, with the only force that had any chance of stopping it gone to ground somewhere.

It was the last thing Shaw wanted to see. He was about to log out of the spy system, defeated and wondering what to do next, when he came upon one last video stream showing the second mystery ship. The G-Net had jumped ahead almost to real-time. It showed the red-stacked ship stopped near the coastline, not far from one of the innermost minor channel islands.

And the weirdest thing about it: In just a few of the frames at the end, it seemed as if some type of very strange, old aircraft was buzzing this ship, maybe even firing at it.

Shaw was stunned. Had the G-Net finally lost its mind? He told it to repeat and go close in on the sequence, hoping that what he was looking at wasn't just another of the cranky spy net's wet dreams.

But once the sequence slowed down and zoomed in, it confirmed Shaw's suspicion. The small plane, flying wildly, and at times apparently out of control, had someone with a gun inside, firing at the ship—this while people on the deck either stood in shock or allowed themselves to get mowed down in the strange strafing run.

This attack lasted only a few frames, and in real-time, maybe forty-five seconds. And the people in the little airplane had managed to do some damage in that short amount of time—leaving the ship's deck spotted with pools of blood. But it fell far short of sinking the freighter. And when this strange bird also began running out of gas, the attack was over.

A few frames later Shaw saw that an unloading operation had begun. Big wooden boxes that appeared to be carrying weapons. That's when the triad of G-Net satellites that had been recording all this began moving out of position. The Earth turning away from them, the satellites went on to other parts of the heavens, leaving Shaw's screen slowly fading to black, like the end of a sad war movie.

The Army officer just sat there for a few moments looking at the blank screen.

What the hell do I do now?

Again, he knew that finding XBat itself would probably be impossible. He knew from past experience that the team could vanish like some kind of strange animal, a chameleon or weird deep sea creature who could put up a such a perfect false front, and blend so well into the landscape, even bloodhounds would have trouble finding them.

But what about the guys in the strange little plane? They had to be connected with XBat. Who the hell else could they have been? Which meant they had to get the little airplane somewhere.

Shaw had the G-Net scan the southern California area for any airports, big or small. He'd expected maybe a dozen, and found there were actually fifty-nine. He didn't want to sit here all day eyeballing all of them, especially since some of the archival images from the Net were over twenty-four hours old.

He just didn't have the time.

He decided instead to concentrate on the small plane itself. Maybe he could find out where it came from.

He asked the G-Net to give him all information on the

small airplane caught in the footage of the brief strafing attack. A few frames reappeared from the black screen. They followed the ghostly fading image as it headed not into shore, but toward a small channel island, actually the nearest landmass. The plane began spouting smoke, and then made a very rapid if controlled descent.

"Out of gas," Shaw mumbled.

The frames ran out after that, but he'd seen enough to come up with at least a plausible theory: He didn't know where XBat was, and it wasn't like he could just call them on the phone. They didn't operate like that.

But this plane—he was sure it came down, either hard or soft, on this small island near Catalina.

Find the people in that plane, he thought, and you'll find XBat.

TEN MINUTES LATER SHAW WAS IN A VERY WINDY parking lot near Venice Beach.

Here, another helicopter was waiting for him, again courtesy of the California Highway Patrol. Shaw groaned when he first saw it. Though he rode in them all the time, he was no big fan of helicopters. Yet he'd requested this one on the QT, and the CHP people had come through. There was no way he could turn it down now.

He'd spent most of the time on the ride down here trying to get in touch with Agent Weir. Shaw nearly expended his cell's battery attempting to raise the CIA agent, as they had previously planned, but for whatever reason, the CIA man was not answering his phone. This was another thing upsetting him. He didn't like being a one-man band, but again, he had no choice. In the search for XBat, he would have to continue on his own.

He thanked his driver and climbed into the bright yellow and blue Sikorsky chopper. Another sheriff's deputy was at the controls. He gave Shaw a quick salute, then held up a map that showed the channel islands, one of them circled in red.

"That's the place," Shaw confirmed.

The pilot pulled up on the controls and off they went.

THEY WERE OVER THE SMALL GROUP OF ISLANDS within fifteen minutes.

The storm was still roaring farther out to sea, with the effects still being felt around these channel islands. The turbulence was scary, and rain showers were blowing very hard through the area. Yet somehow the copter pilot managed to fight his way through all the atmospherics, and soon Shaw found himself looking down at the island in question. He knew right away, though, it might not be a pleasant mission.

The pilot was the first to see it. He simply tapped Shaw on the knee and pointed to a spot slightly to the northwest.

"Wreckage," was all he said.

They were over it in seconds—or at least the largest part of it. It was the fuselage of the strange little Sperryman biplane. It was twisted and smoldering, hanging in a large willow-type tree. A little bit beyond was the engine still in its cowling, burning like an unexploded bomb in a clearing near the willow grove.

The biplane's wings were just a few yards beyond that. They too were twisted and burning, the smoke mixing easily with the rain and fog hiding the island. Shaw had visited many airplane crash sites in his time with the DIA. From the looks of this one, there were no survivors.

The funny little plane had crashed on the tiny unoccupied island nearly an hour ago. Knowing Autry's guys, if they had survived, they would have been out on the open beach by now with signal flares or warning smoke, or laying out pieces of the wreckage in a message that could be read from above. Autry's guys were so gung-ho, so highly trained and motivated, so *involved*, Shaw knew they would do anything in their power to get off that island and back into the fight. *If* they were still alive.

But seeing none of this kind of activity below, Shaw believed his worst fears were being confirmed. Whoever had been aboard the odd little plane had died in the crash.

That's when he heard the pilot say the one word he really didn't want to hear: "Bodies . . ."

Shaw felt his heart hit his feet. "Where?"

He was searching the sands below him but could see nothing out of the ordinary.

The pilot nudged him and pointed not down at the ground, but to the water, specifically the rough wave-tossed surface on the eastern edge of the island. Sure enough, Shaw could see two bodies about two hundred feet offshore.

Had they been thrown from the crash? Or had they tried to jump out before the plane went in? There was no way of telling.

All that was clear was that two figures were floating in the choppy waters. It had to be Autry's guys.

But then . . . something very strange. Though he couldn't have sworn to it, Shaw thought he saw one of the bodies move its arms. And then the other did as well. And now their legs were moving too. The pilot turned toward the two figures in an instant. The closer the copter got, the clearer the situation became.

Shaw couldn't believe it. The two in the water were definitely wearing XBat's trademark black uniform. But they weren't dead. They had survived the crash. And they'd wanted to get back into the fight so much that despite the storm and the waves and the wind and the rain, they were *swimming* to the mainland.

The pilot just shook his head.

"Man," he said, slowing down for a mid-sea pickup. "Those guys are *dedicated* . . ."

CHAPTER 15

THE COCKPIT OF THE TEXTRON HAD CRASHED INTO AN alley squeezed between two elderly skyscrapers off La Brea Avenue.

It had been a long way down. Seconds after the missile hit the copter, the stricken aircraft went into a violent spin. Weir was thrown against the side window again, this time breaking his nose. Though dazed and alarmed, he could still see roving bands of demonstrators looking up at him as the copter plunged to the ground.

Just how Alberto managed not to hit either of the thirty-story buildings, Weir would never know. The pilot wrestled with the controls all the whole way down, pushing the Textron this way and that, alternately slamming both of them against their seats and then against the control panel and back against their seats again.

The last thing Weir remembered was looking down at his hands and realizing they were covered with blood. Was it his? Was he already bleeding? Or did he pick it up when he was moving Dana's body? He couldn't remember.

The copter crashed just a second later.

Everything went black after that.

WEIR AWOKE SOMETIME LATER. IT COULD HAVE BEEN minutes, it could have been hours. He couldn't tell. His face was covered in blood now—and this time he knew it was his own.

What was left of the helicopter was up on top of him. He was trapped, his legs pinned between the seat and the flight console. Both were broken. His hands were also burnt, and most of his clothes had been torn away. But he was alive. That was the biggest surprise of all.

Alberto had not been so lucky. The pilot was still at the controls, his face drained of blood, dead white, staring over at Weir. In this nightmare in slow motion, it dawned on the CIA man that the pilot had saved his life—at the cost of his own.

It took a while for Weir to wipe the blood from his eyes. Only then did he discover he was not alone in the alley. There were masked protesters all around him. Some were gathered at the south end of the alley next to a burning delivery truck, staring in at him. Over the concrete wall to his east, several dozen more were over-turning cars and smashing windows; they'd also spotted him. Most strange, there were protesters standing out on an ancient-looking atrium hanging off the nearest building, five stories up. These people were armed with rifles and were firing wildly at some target out of Weir's field of view.

Again, all this seemed like a dream to him. A bad dream. The surreal aspects were overwhelming. The chaos all around him. Alberto's death stare. His own injuries, bloody certainly, maybe even serious. Worst of all, he couldn't move his legs; the twisted metal of the copter's wreckage had him caught like an animal in a trap.

As his head cleared somewhat, he realized the noise around him was deafening. Sirens, dozens of them, explosions, car horns blaring, people screaming, shouting, the crackle of flames—and above it all, the sickening sound of gunfire. Weir had been in many combat situations before, but nothing like this. He'd fallen into a battle zone—right in the middle of America's second largest city.

Strange place to die, he thought.

He shut his eyes and felt the tears come. Had this happened to him in Kenya or Baghdad, or Kosovo or Tashkent—it wouldn't have been nearly as bad. At least he would have died doing what he'd done all his life: protecting his country from somewhere overseas. But to go like this, while Los Angeles was being torn apart? He would have never predicted his end would be so weird.

His wife. His kids. He would never see them again. And he'd failed in his last mission. He'd allowed a mole to get into the resort, within the perimeter. A mole who had already killed, and was obviously not shy about killing again. And his target? No less than the President of the United States; Weir was certain of it. And it was all his fault.

So, maybe it was better that he go now.

No sooner had this thought taken hold than he started hearing more disturbing sounds. Above the cacophony going on around him came the disheartening racket of bullets pinging off the smoldering wreckage of the Textron.

His eyes open wide now, Weir looked up to see the armed protesters on the atrium overhead firing down at him. But this was not all. The demonstrators in the open space to his east were also shooting at him.

"Bastards!" he managed to croak, but that's about all he could get out. His throat suddenly felt as if it were on fire. He somehow got his fingers up near his Adam's Apple and discovered he was bleeding from there too.

That's when he saw another group of protesters coming down the alley. They were carrying weapons as well, but two were also armed with spray paint. One protester spray-painted "Anarchy's Reign" on a wall not twenty feet away from him.

"*Ignorant* bastards!" Weir managed to gurgle.

Whether they heard him or not, the rebuke brought more gunfire in his direction. And this time the pings of small caliber ammunition were replaced with the gut-wrenching crash of 30mm rounds and larger. Military weapons.

The second cargo ship, Weir thought. It must have gotten through. And it must have been carrying weapons too. And just as he had suspected before they crashed, now those weapons were washing through the streets of L.A.

He found himself whispering something he'd learned years before in finishing school, in Latin class: *"Mundus fini . . ."* It is the end of the world.

He tried one last time to free himself, but it was no use. In seconds the armed men were swarming all over the wreckage. He could feel a fury coming off them. A hate . . . He saw hands reaching toward him but then suddenly stop. Maybe it was because he was so bloody, or that he was trapped, or that they were saving him for last—whatever the reason, they stepped right over him, grabbed Alberto's lifeless body and laughingly dragged it down the alley and into the street beyond.

Weir went crazy. He had only one arm free but he started punching those protesters remaining near him. Several of them jumped back and fell away from the wreckage—indeed they'd thought he was dead and had suddenly come back to life. Whatever fucked-up drugs were going through their systems caused many of them to freak out. Some even ran away.

But others drew nearer—and these people were wearing both ski masks and red kerchiefs. They were also carrying AK-47s. They realized they had a live one on their hands. Now even more hands went to grab for him. They began yanking Weir out of wreckage, not stopping first to free his legs from the twisted metal. The pain was excruciating. He was being ripped in half.

Then more bullets came crashing down around him—but now something had changed. The hands trying to dismember him began falling away. Smoke clogged his bloody throat. More flashes. More cracks of rifle fire. More screaming.

All the hands clutching at him were suddenly gone. The smoke blew away, the screaming faded. He heard the sound of feet running back down the alley. The gunfire continued, though; if anything, if became louder. Yet none of the bullets had hit him. He'd expected the fatal shot at any moment. But it never came.

When he opened his eyes again, he saw why.

Two L.A. sheriff's deputies, in full SWAT gear and armed with M-15s, had jumped into the alley. Their gunfire had scattered the protesters, and they were still firing at the hastily retreating thugs.

One of them reached back and held his hand against Weir's throat. "Are you still alive?" he asked.

Weir tried to say *I think so.*

But no words would come out. Whatever kind of wound he had in his throat, he couldn't speak. And because his hands were burned and bleeding, he couldn't write. So while the deputies had saved his life, what good was it? There was no way he could tell them about the mole at the resort, especially in the middle of the revived gun battle. No way to make them understand.

This crushing frustration almost killed him right then and there.

Suddenly a new storm of bullets rained down on them. One of the deputies threw his body over Weir, firing his weapon at the same time. The gunfire was coming from both the atrium five stories up and the clutch of armed protesters who had taken up a new position at the far end of the alley. In seconds more than thirty people were shooting at them.

The gun battle, such as it was, lasted only a minute. The deputy who had protected Weir took two bullets to the head, under his helmet and through his visor. He died in an instant, his body continuing to shield the CIA agent. In an attempt to see if his colleague was still alive, the second deputy tried crawling toward the back of the wreckage. It was a valiant effort but proved to be a fatal one. As soon the man began moving, the gunmen up on the atrium fired down on him. A great splash of bullets hit him all at once, flattening him. There was a spray of blood; the deputy let out a loud groan and died immediately.

And just like that, Weir was alone again.

He couldn't believe it. Just like his copter pilot, these two men, unknown to him, had given their lives just to save his.

And for what?

He lay back again and begged for the end. Whispered on his bloody lips, his lesson from Latin class.

Mundus fini.

The end of the world . . .

CHAPTER 16

Grape River Air Field

BOBBY AUTRY WAS ASLEEP WHEN THE KNOCK CAME
at the door.

He thought it was in his dream—a mishmash of being
alone in his Black Hawk strafing a toy boat in a typical
family bathtub—and then someone was knocking on
the bathroom door.

He woke up just in time to hear Sheriff Kemp say,
"Who goes there?" A phrase no one had used in thirty
years.

The reply came back a bit uncertain, "Cliffside Police
Department . . ."

This made all of XBat sit up and take notice. Sheriff
Kemp, who had spent the time guarding the unit while
still keeping up with his blogging, finally logged off and
pulled the door open.

The two Cliffside cops walked in—and right behind

them was a man dressed in a very natty military uniform.

Autry couldn't believe it. It was Jim Shaw.

Shaw smartly saluted Sheriff Kemp, and before the lawman could saw a word, was shaking his hand.

"You have my gratitude," he told the sheriff in a very confident, even boastful way. "Thanks for watching over these mugs. I'll take it from here."

Kemp enthusiastically returned the salute and the handshake, but then looked the Army officer up and down.

"Who are you?" he asked Shaw, as the two Cliffside cops stood by mutely.

Shaw hastily introduced himself then pulled out three ID cars. CIA, DIA, and Homeland Security.

"Take your pick," he told Kemp. "We've got bad things happening up north. That's why I came to get these guys. Their aircraft are needed."

Still Kemp sniffed the possibility that he was getting railroaded.

"I'm not saying that I don't want to take your word for it," he told Shaw. "But how do I really know you are who you say you are?"

Sheriff Kemp still had his gun, and the Cliffside cops, whom Shaw had intercepted just as they were approaching the hangar, had not been disarmed either. To do so would have ruined Shaw's ruse. But now all three of the lawmen were looking skeptical and fingering their weapons.

Shaw kept his cool. Though his enormous Magnum handgun was not far from his reach, he knew the perfect solution to this sudden complication. He reached inside his jacket and pulled out not the massive handgun, but the wad of bills he'd withdrawn for the bank.

He peeled off five $1,000 bills and held them up in front of Kemp.

"This is payment for the gasoline," Shaw said, literally stuffing the bills into Kemp's pocket.

He turned to the two Cliffside cops and peeled off another $5,000 each. "And this is for your time," he said. "And your trouble."

The three lawmen were so stunned, they didn't even notice that Shaw had given Autry the high sign and that XBat was slowly getting to their feet. With no words spoken, they simply walked out of the open hangar door into the shitty weather beyond.

Shaw shook hands with the three startled but pleasantly surprised law men. It was smiles all around now. The two cops even saluted him. But Shaw left them with one last thought.

"Now seriously, nothing ever happened here, boys," he said in a tone that left nothing uncertain. "It's all top secret and it's best we keep it that way."

To make his point, he pulled out another ID card from his collection. This one identified him as being employed by the NSA.

"Because if you guys ever breathe a word of any of this," he concluded with a smile, holding the NSA card

up to eye level. "Well, let's just say, 'We'll be listening . . .'"

IT TOOK XBAT ONLY TWENTY MINUTES TO FUEL UP
and get airborne again.

Autry was back in the driver's seat of his DAP Black
Hawk. Zucker was his copilot. In the jump seat behind
them was Major Shaw, still no fan of helicopter rides.

It took Shaw a couple minutes to update the unit on
what had happened during their brief incarceration.
L.A. was in chaos. Despite the efforts of Mungo and
McCune, the second freighter had already unloaded its
weapons cargo, and those weapons had probably found
their way into Los Angeles by now. Plus, since meeting
with Weir under the Hollywood sign, Shaw had not
been able to contact the CIA agent.

All this added up to a security nightmare for L.A. and
for the WTO meeting. That's why Shaw was ordering
XBat to Los Angeles.

The unit formed up over Grape River and turned as
one toward L.A. Even from here they could see a pall
of smoke rising over the city. But for Autry, hearing that
Weir was incommunicado was a more troubling piece of
news. Weir was *always* reachable, if the person calling
knew where to call. In a dire situation like this, for him
to be out of touch was just plain weird.

Even as they were rushing to L.A., Autry urged Shaw
to try the CIA agent's cell phone again. But Shaw got

no reply, just as he'd been getting since trying to contact Weir hours ago.

So Autry tried to call Weir on his own cell phone instead. Incredibly, someone answered on the second ring.

"Can you get me out of here?" the voice on the other end was pleading.

"Who is this?" Autry replied, knowing immediately it was not Weir.

What followed was a rambling, disconcerting conversation that Autry finally realized was coming from an office worker who was stuck in an alley in L.A., trapped by the violence all around him and desperate to get rescued.

Autry calmed the guy down, knowing he had to ascertain what was going on around this person. He started by asking the frightened office worker how he got Weir's cell phone in the first place. The story he heard was extremely troubling.

The office worker had witnessed Weir's helicopter being shot down, and related how the pilot had somehow managed to land the stricken craft between the two skyscrapers just off La Brea. The office worker reported seeing two bodies still in the wreckage—but said they were sheriff's deputies who'd come to the aid of the crash victims only to be shot by the protesters. Then, while they were dragging the pilot's body through the streets, someone else badly injured in the crash but still alive was taken away by the assailants. Only when the alley was empty again did the office worker emerge from one of the skyscrapers to find Weir's cell phone in the wreckage.

"I think they took this injured guy to the bank around the corner," he said. "There are a lot of those assholes in there."

Before Autry could ask another question, he heard the unmistakable crack of gunfire in the background.

After that, the cell phone went dead.

THE FLOW OF BLOOD INTO GARY WEIR'S EYES HAD not stopped. It was still dribbling down from the gash across his brow, and from the multitude of other cuts and abrasions he had on top of his head.

His left arm was hanging useless at his side. It was broken about halfway between his elbow and shoulder; it was bleeding heavily as well. His right arm was still working, more or less. It was filled with dozens of glass slivers from the control panel that exploded when the copter crashed. He'd somehow sustained a bloody injury in his throat as well.

It was his legs he was most worried about, though. The protesters had dragged him from the wreckage, this after pouring dozens of rounds into the two deputies who'd saved his life. That his legs were still attached to his body seemed like a miracle in itself; that's how roughly the protesters had handled him. But while his legs were bleeding heavily, he had lost all feeling in them. Dead weight from his groin down. Was he paralyzed? Just in shock? With every breath, he thought he could feel life itself slowly draining out of him.

His captors had carried him into the first floor of the building next to the alley. From what Weir could see through his addled eyes, the place looked like some kind of bank or credit union. All the windows were broken. All the furniture had been shot up. A couple of minor fires were smoldering in the corner. There was blood splattered all over the rug as well, and through his limited vision, Weir saw at least three dead LAPD cops. His hazy instinct told him they'd come in here seeking refuge, but the mob found them instead. Their bodies had been unceremoniously dumped in the bank's lobby.

Though there were many protesters moving in and out of the building, all of them carrying heavy weapons, Weir found it impossible to count them all. At least three dozen, maybe many more. They were all sporting AK-47s and/or RPG launchers. Some were wearing bandoleers holding hand grenades or long ammo belts. Weir almost laughed. The LAPD had been armed to the ass for this protest, but only with riot gear. They didn't count on the WTO protesters having heavy weapons, or any weapons at all. Like the infamous L.A. bank robbery in 1997, when two heavily armed gunmen shot up half of a neighborhood trying to make their escape, facing LAPD officers with little more than their service revolvers. Those two criminals had wreaked havoc on L.A. for hours that day. Now it was as if an entire army of these characters had descended on the City of Angels—overwhelming the LAPD and sending them running. Unthinkable, but true.

But it was the armed men themselves who fascinated Weir—in a very dark way. Each one had a ski mask covering his head, plus a red or black kerchief as an additional covering for the lower part of the face. Double protection from being identified. Even in his seriously wounded condition, Weir became obsessed with finding out just who these people were.

He'd known a little about the typical WTO demonstrator. They were usually anarchists, or against world government, and they could be a destructive lot. They'd ruined downtown Seattle back in the 1990s, smashing storefront windows, setting places afire, battling police and generally trashing anything that could be trashed. Similar outbursts had taken place in other cities that had hosted the WTO, like Montreal.

But those people hadn't come armed—and certainly not with the combat weapons Weir had seen in evidence here. He had no doubts now that these weapons had come from the second mystery freighter, the one that got away. That the first cargo ship had been sunk by XBat was a small comfort. The heavy-duty weapons that Shaw had reported on that ship could have lain waste to blocks of L.A. had they made it to the streets. So in a strange way, the problem was only half as bad as it could have been, thanks to Autry's guys.

But half as bad was bad enough.

It's come to our shores finally, he thought, the words spinning around his head. Like 9/11, nothing will ever be the same again.

But *who* were they? Who were these masked men intent on ripping the very fabric of America in two? Try as he might, Weir did not see one without a mask, and certainly he had no opportunity to look up under one. They were covered and they were faceless—and maybe that was the point. Maybe it didn't make any difference who they were. Maybe these phantoms were just the ghosts of America's darker past, coming back to haunt it. For committing the sin of keeping the poor in their place, Los Angeles was now amuck with criminals, running wild and pissing on what was left of the American dream. A less than comforting last thought. Or then again, maybe they represented something else entirely.

They had put him into the bank's small vault, closing the iron gate but not the vault door itself. He was slumped against the wall now, feeling like a broken doll, his mind going in and out of shock. He tried to conjure up a picture of his wife and kids one last time in his mind, at the same moment wondering just how long it would take before he bled to death.

But just before he slipped into unconsciousness, he heard a strange rumbling noise.

Far off, but getting closer.

He thought it sounded like helicopters.

CHAPTER 17

BY 10:30 A.M. THE SMOKE COMING OVER THE TREES AT
Briar Patch had become so thick it was blotting out the
sun.

From the vantage point of the ultra exclusive resort, it
seemed half of Los Angeles was on fire. Worse, the spare
reports they were getting from the LAPD indicated that
the situation inside the city was out of control, that the
police force was suddenly "ineffective" and that large
numbers of demonstrators were heading for Beverly
Hills unchecked.

Senior agent Fred Haas was in charge of the Secret
Service detail at Briar Patch. While the situation had
deteriorated so rapidly it had been almost humanly impossible to keep up with, by ten-thirty, he knew he had
to get the President out. Though he was loath to be seen
beating a hasty retreat, especially in an American city,
he would have to leave it to the spinmeisters to sort out
the ramifications. Anarchy running wild in the streets of

L.A., just blocks from where the President was hosting the most powerful men in the world? It wasn't the Secret Service's job to worry about that. They were here to keep the Chief Executive safe. That's what they had to do.

Standing in the parking lot located next to the meeting hall, Haas consulted with his two senior men. They too agreed it was time to go—and that in the interest of expediency, they would not inform the other myriad security agencies on the scene of their decision. This was a small matter. If everything went well, by the time anyone knew what happened, the POTUS would already be gone.

Haas had a very high-tech cell phone called a CSP at his disposal; government-speak for Communicator, Secure, Personal. It was the device on which all Secret Service people talked to each other. He now punched a code into the CSP. This sent a message directly to the Secret Service agent inside the meeting hall, where the WTO conference was just getting under way. It would be up to this agent to pass a note to the POTUS telling him that the Secret Service had found the situation unsafe and that he would have to leave.

This message sent, Haas punched another code into the CSP. It went directly to the crew chief of *Marine One*, the president's helicopter, which was parked out on the fairway near the ninth hole, about five hundred feet away. The message was equally stark and unambiguous: *Get ready for an emergency egress. We're getting out.*

The Marine crew chief was quickly up in the cockpit. He passed the message on to the two pilots. They immediately quick-started the helicopters' twin engines. An instant later the aircraft's huge rotors began to spin.

The helicopter had only been on the ground for twenty minutes. It had arrived almost unseen just about the same time the POTUS made his grand entrance in the top-secret VTOL aircraft. It had been followed here by a second identical copter, a backup in case something went wrong with the first. The second copter was also parked near the ninth hole.

Again, it was just five hundred feet to the top of the resort's main parking lot; this was the designated emergency pickup spot for the presidential helicopter. It was secure enough for the copter to set down for the few seconds it would take to hustle the Chief Executive aboard. This would be followed by what was known as an all-engine clear-out climb to the right. Translated: the fastest way possible to get the hell out of Briar Patch.

Because it was a specially built copter, *Marine One* was able to get airborne after just a minute of engine warm-up. Some standard copters took nearly five times as long before they could take off. This quick launch technique brought an astounding amount of heat to the aircraft's engines in a short amount of time. Only once it was airborne would the engines have enough influx of air to cool down properly. But again, the copter was made for just these things.

The pilots watched their control settings continue to

rise. Finally, at fifty-five seconds, they were ready to go. They would lift the copter up to a hundred feet and slowly drift over to the parking lot. At the same time, the Secret Service crew would bring the Chief Executive out to the landing site. The copter would descend slowly, just barely kissing the parking lot while their cargo was put aboard. Then they would be off for good.

Both pilots checked their engines' temperature. It was high, but that was OK. Then all was set. They gave each other a nod and the pilot pulled up on the aircraft's collective control. *Marine One* began to rise slowly into the smoky air.

Haas and his two senior officers were watching from the parking lot, timing their move to whisk the Chief Executive out of the meeting room to the landing site. A bounce-back from the agent inside the meeting hall confirmed that the POTUS had been informed of the decision to leave, and while he OK'd it, it really wasn't his decision to make. The rest of the WTO leaders, no doubt startled at the President's pending quick exit, had been brought back into another secure room deeper inside the resort and told, disingenuously, that other arrangements were being made for their exits as well.

The CSP communicator now got a corresponding beep from *Marine One*, confirming that the copter was off the ground. It was time to usher the Chief Executive out of the building. As soon as the copter was down on the parking lot's asphalt surface, they would lift the POTUS aboard and then two of them would join him.

The third man, the less senior of the staff, would remain behind at the resort and help the other world leaders get out, if that was even possible now.

Marine One reached its hundred feet in altitude. As planned, it started a slow sideways drift over to the parking area. Suddenly, out of the smoke and dust, a flash of light . . . Then a streak of fire crossed the length of the golf course. A missile . . . Attracted by the hyperheat coming from the helicopter's quick-start engines, it went right over the meeting hall, across the tree line, and smashed into the side of *Marine One*.

There was another bright flash of light, blinding as it lit up the smoky sky. Then a huge explosion, with a shock wave that went across the fairway, up the hill and into the meeting room, shattering several of its huge windows. The three Secret Service men hit the ground and covered up from the storm of broken glass. When they were able to look up again, they saw the presidential helicopter hanging in the air for a long moment, aflame from one end to the other. Then it simply fell—right on top of *Marine Two*, its twin aircraft—and exploded again. A huge fireball erupted and climbed into the sky, dissolving into a mushroom of thick black smoke.

When the dust cleared there was nothing left of the two presidential helicopters but twin smoking holes in the ground.

*   *   *

McCUNE'S WAS THE FIRST XBAT COPTER TO ARRIVE over L.A.

Soaking wet, but feeling none of the effects of his long swim, he was back flying the unit's command aircraft. The big Chinook was stuffed with high-tech navigation and communications gear, essentially the unit's AWACs craft. As such, McCune was like the scout in front of the cavalry. And at the moment, "Indian Country" was downtown L.A.

He put the command copter into a circle high above the corner of La Brea and Bradley. He was trying to do many things at once. He was flying the big Chinook, he was watching the chaos unfold on the streets below, and also monitoring the radio conversations with the rest of XBat just a mile behind him.

A brief radio message from Autry moments before told McCune that there were portable SAMs on the ground below. At least two had been fired at Weir's Textron copter, about thirty minutes ago. One of them had hit their mark. This was how McCune and the rest of the unit learned that the CIA agent's tricked-out copter had been shot down.

This was not good. On hearing the SAM report, McCune immediately ordered his guys in back to crank up the Chinook's own air defense suite. The device—actually a collection of sensors—would tell him if any airborne threats were about to bring harm to him or anyone in XBat.

In the meantime McCune overheard a radio conver-

sation between Autry and his passenger, Major Shaw.
They'd also learned where Weir had been shot down, as a
person who'd found Weir's his cell phone had given them
the exact location before meeting an uncertain fate. They
also knew that someone had been carried away from the
crash, injured but alive, possibly Weir himself.

But these things didn't add up for Shaw the same
way they did for XBat, and especially Autry. For Shaw
this meant that brave as he was, Weir was just another
casualty, and probably a fatality, one of many on this
apocalyptic day. It was a sickening thought that it
might even be Weir's body the protesters were dragging
through the streets—but this was war now, and people
died brutally in war. It was just a shame that Weir had
to be one of them.

Autry, though, saw it the exact opposite way. The
unit had worked so closely with Weir in the past year
they considered him one of their own. And the motto
of XBat, as well as all of TF-160, was simple: "No one
gets left behind."

So while Shaw wanted XBat to get to Briar Patch
immediately to help with security there, Autry told him
the unit had one thing to do first. They had to try to
rescue Weir.

In the conversation that everyone in XBat could hear
via their radio channels, when Shaw asked, "Isn't the
President of the United States more important right
now than Agent Weir?" Autry replied, "At this moment, no."

That brought cheers to all of the team's helicopters. But then they got down to business. They had a rescue mission to run.

Which was why McCune was trying his best to keep aware of the chaos in the streets in downtown L.A. The team was going to have to land down there very soon—and to his eyes, it looked as hostile as anything he'd seen in Iraq.

He was also trying to monitor the situation up at Briar Patch, which was about ten miles to his north. He could hear scattered radio transmissions and cell phone traffic coming from the resort. It sounded panicky, with a high level of concern coming through via both mediums. McCune could also see hordes of demonstrators peeling off from the main packs and running headlong up toward Briar Patch. At the same time, though, he could see groups of LAPD officers who had previously surrounded the compound simply melting away. Was this just a bad coincidence—the cops leaving the one area that needed protection more then ever—or was it a brilliant feint by the demonstrators, whoever they were, to draw the cops away from their main target at the worst possible time?

"What a freaking mess," McCune whispered to himself.

He looked back down at his defensive suite. So far, so good. He could see flares and fireworks shooting up all over the city, perfect cover for any shoulder-launched antiaircraft missiles that might be preparing to fire down there. But as for the real thing, there was nothing yet.

Should a SAM be launched at his Chinook, the rowdy pilot knew what to do: dispense red-hot distraction flares, crank up the copter's substantial ECM electronic interference system, and push the big copter over on its side, falling away from any on-coming missile. McCune had performed this evasion tactic more than once in his career with TF-160. But never did he think he'd be considering such a thing over an American city.

The other copters in XBat finally arrived. They went into a slow circle above the two old skyscrapers where Weir's copter reportedly went in. McCune put the Chinook into another tight break, going down very low and sweeping an eye over everything within blocks of the designated rescue area. The streets were filled with burning cars, burning buildings, and hundreds of people running wild. But how many of them were actually *armed?* There was just no way he could tell.

McCune immediately sent a message to Autry's Black Hawk, reporting all this. He added that if XBat was going to land and search for Weir, they'd better do it now and in a hurry, and be prepared to go in "hot." Autry acknowledged the message and then radioed the four other XBat Black Hawks. In seconds they had formed up in a landing pattern and begun to descend on the city.

Suddenly McCune's air defense suite came to life. The warning buzzer was the last sound he wanted to hear, but a quick glance of the readouts told him this was not a SAM rising up to strike him or any of the other copters in XBat. Instead, his long range radar scanner was showing a much larger blip, coming not from the ground below, but the skies to the east. And it was moving fast.

"What the fuck is this?" he swore to himself.

He called back to his electronics threat officer. This man's equipment had ultra long range TV capability; by using the Galaxy Net, he could see just about anything flying within a fifty-mile radius of them. The airspace over L.A. had been closed as soon as the police saw SAMs flying up from the ground. So what was causing this image?

It was not a copter or an airliner or a small private plane, the electronics threat officer finally reported. But it was carrying weapons. Armed weapons—and lots of them.

"What the hell is it then?" McCune called back to him.

The electronics threat officer turned a few dials and punched a few touch panels.

Then he replied: "My best guess? I'd say it's an A-10 attack plane. And it's heading right for us."

JEROME HAD REACHED HIS FIRST OBJECTIVE.

It was called MGM Square. It was located in the middle of downtown L.A., a four-block area festooned with skyscrapers, some modern, others right out of the 1960s.

Nearly all of Jerome's men had made it here as well. The three tractor trailer trucks had penetrated L.A. unmolested as far as the end of Wilshire. There, obstacles police had put in the roadway prevented them from going any farther. No matter—the men simply poured out of the trucks, skirted the police position and began walking northwest, toward MGM Square.

They'd fired a few RPG rounds along the way—randomly blowing up several cars and demolishing several small businesses—just to see if the RPGs actually worked. In all cases, the smuggled weaponry performed perfectly.

The same was true with the Stinger teams. Though they'd been dispersed throughout the city, they'd shot down at least one helicopter so far. In fact, the stricken craft had crashed right behind the building Jerome was now using as a regrouping point. And by dumb luck or just dark fate, he and his men had determined that this particular helicopter, tricked out and jammed with high-tech navigation and defensive gear, belonged to none other than the CIA. This was very interesting to "Douglas," the man running the entire operation. When Jerome reported the discovery to him, via another sanitized cell phone, Douglas replied that, at all costs, anyone left alive aboard the Textron should be taken alive and kept alive as long as possible. That's how Jerome had come by his first prisoner, the battered passenger in the copter, at present locked in the bank's vault room. However, the man was so severely injured, he doubted he could last more than another half hour, though he refrained from telling this to Douglas.

Jerome knew other teams armed with assault rifles and hand grenades were already operating throughout the city. Like his own Stinger teams, theirs was a different mission. They were here to shoot at cops. But for Jerome and his RPG men, it was all about fucking up L.A. itself—and doing it with more than bullets and frags.

Of the four hundred RPGs they'd set out with, more than 385 were still left. Again, those that had been expended were shot at high quality, high damage targets along the way. But this place, MGM Square, was Jerome's real target. The home to many of L.A.'s biggest banks and moneyed corporations, it was the financial heart of the city. His orders were to rip it out.

No sooner had he and his men regrouped in the first floor of the partially burned-out bank than Jerome began doing just that. Sending out his RPG teams in all directions, his orders to them remained simple: If it looks expensive, blow it up.

Shortly after his arrival, he received a call from another cell of people armed with AK-47s. They were just a block away, ready to hold off anyone who tried to interfere with what Jerome was doing. In other words, his protection had arrived as well. But Jerome was confident they would not be necessary. The L.A. cops were running for their lives.

No one was going to bother him here.

But no sooner did these thoughts go through his head than he heard a great rumbling. It was so loud the air itself seemed to be shaking.

Jerome looked out the bank's crumbled facade to see five helicopters go right over the square. And these were not police helicopters; they were all black and had weapons sticking out of them everywhere. They were descending rapidly, as if planning to land just a block away.

Jerome couldn't believe it.

"What the fuck is this?" he bellowed. *"Who the fuck are these guys?"*

BOBBY AUTRY'S BLACK HAWK WAS DOWN ON THE street less than ten seconds before he realized he was surrounded.

The four Black Hawks, plus his own, had landed at the end of Bradley Avenue, just before the intersection with Santa Monica. They'd come in via a very tight formation, something they'd trained to do many times over. Packed tight was the best way to approach a landing zone in any dense urban area, where space was usually at a premium.

But this part of Bradley had been covered with debris and trash long before XBat showed up; even worse, a large dump truck carrying road sand had been set upon by the protesters here and flipped over in the early stages of the riot, spreading sand and ash everywhere. So when the unit descended, there was so much smoke and dust and confusion, all whipped up by the five copter rotors, it was like landing with a blindfold on. And though the XBat troops stood ready to pile out of their aircraft, in accordance with the assault plan, in truth none of them could see more than ten feet in front of him.

It was only when some of the dust finally began to clear that Autry realized they'd set down in the middle of a large group of demonstrators, many of whom had been hidden in the numerous doorways up and down this block of Bradley Avenue. Most fled at the first sight of the copters, descending in slow motion like invaders from another world. Others just stood by frozen as the heavily armed flying machines appeared in their midst.

The copters weren't staying long. Autry gave the order and the troops began jumping out of their aircraft. He unstrapped himself, grabbed his M-16 and quickly joined them on the windy, debris-strewn L.A. street. No sooner had his boots touched the ground than Zucker lifted Autry's copter back up into the air. Followed by the four other Black Hawks, they all ascended to the relative safety of 250 feet.

That's when the gunfire started.

It seemed to come from every direction all at once. Steams of tracers and frag grenades. A storm of fire and lead had suddenly come down on top of XBat.

Autry's troopers scrambled to the best cover possible: the doorways of the skyscrapers that populated this part of L.A., the same ones vacated by the frightened demonstrators seconds before. Here, they started firing back, and the next ten seconds was indescribable. Tracers were flying everywhere, explosions going off—the noise was tremendous.

Five troopers never made it to cover. They were immediately cut down in the street. But this was where XBat's amazing training and ability came through. No sooner had these five troopers hit the pavement when one of the Black Hawks who'd just delivered the men was suddenly back again. Its pilots had seen everything and simply reacted, the trademark of XBat's success in tight situations. The Black Hawk troop ship bounced back down long enough for other troopers to load the five wounded men onto it and then, in another roar of dust and sand, it was gone again, straight up and out of danger.

The wounded men had not lain in the street more than ten seconds.

This piece of gallantry had caused a pause in the incoming fire. It started up again almost immediately, though. Autry and five of his men had found cover in the entranceway of the Pacific Textiles building. They immediately went into their best defensive position. The streaks of tracers going in both directions had become blinding now, so intense was the gun battle. Autry wiped the sweat from his brow and checked his watch. They'd been on the ground less than a minute.

He'd prayed for an unopposed landing—foolishly, as

it turned out. Deep down inside, Autry had hoped they wouldn't have to shoot at anyone once on the ground. The thought of killing other Americans was just about the worst thing he could conceive of—assuming the people firing at them *were* Americans.

But now it really didn't matter. These people were heavily armed and they'd fired at his men, and now his men were firing back.

He knew the ramifications would be huge, especially since there was a chance that he and his guys were no longer official military troops. But whoever the hell they were, these gunmen and their confederates had done extensive damage to this part of L.A. already. Autry hoped that was enough justification—for his superiors, for the fate of his men, for the fate of his own psyche—for him to return fire.

But if XBat had any hope of making it out of the ambush intact, it also had to be done the right away. Autry keyed his head mic, opening up a channel inside the helmet of every other guy in XBat.

"Hold your fire," was his first order, then: "Spotter teams, initiate cluster-target IDs."

All fire from the top secret copter unit ceased immediately. Huddled in the glass and steel doorways, the men of XBat went into observation mode, noting the location of every flash they could see from an AK-47. As it turned out, most of the enemy gunfire was coming from the lower floors of the buildings all around them. In fact, it was coming down on them now like a torrent.

Unlike their unseen enemy, though, XBat wasn't about uncontrolled fire. The every-man-for-himself style of gunfight only worked in movies. XBat knew better. Even as the enemy gunfire intensified, spotters in each of XBat's five squads began pinpointing firing sources by sweeping their rifle-mounted IR sighting devices across the lower floors of the buildings around them and looking for sources of heat, like muzzle flashes. This information—known as target cluster IDs—was then flashed to the IR sights of every other trooper in the unit, with each location prioritized. All this happened in a matter of seconds.

In this way, and in this small time frame, the XBat troopers were suddenly all on the same page. They knew who to shoot at first. Target cluster number one: the third floor of the building located at the corner of Bradley and Davis. At least a half-dozen gunmen were up there. Everyone in XBat who had a clear shot pointed his weapon in that direction.

On Autry's call, more than three dozen weapons opened up on this one spot. M-16s, M-50s, grenade launchers, even a few shotguns. It all hit the enemy gun post like a gigantic fiery hand. Delivered with the fury of an artillery barrage, *this* was concentrated fire, XBat-style. It lasted just three seconds. When the smoke cleared, nearly a quarter of the building's third floor had been blown away.

Target cluster number two was right across the street from number one. An odd building, it was only five stories high. At least a dozen gunmen were firing at XBat from the top floor windows. Pretty much the same thing happened next. Target acquired, target fired upon. Long rows of tracers, the sparkle of 50-caliber fire. The fiery *whomp!* of the grenade launchers going off. A five-second barrage at most—nothing more was needed. The smoke blew itself away down Davis Avenue, revealing that the entire fifth floor of the small building had been vaporized.

Target clusters three and four were handled the same way. Every trooper in the unit knowing the next target, every one pointing his muzzle in that direction and then letting go for four or five heartbeats. Concentrated firepower—the secret of how to win a street fight. Already, the enemy fire was dropping off.

But there was a slight problem. The two remaining target clusters were on roofs of nearby buildings that were too high for XBat's weapons to reach.

No matter. All of the XBat copters were flying in a wide circle above the madness, their pilots listening in on what was happening on the ground below.

Two of the DAPs peeled off from the group and streaked right down the middle of Davis Boulevard. They spilt up right over Autry's head, one headed toward each of the remaining target clusters.

Weapons were engaged, rockets fired. Two more buildings were quickly missing their roofs. It happened that fast. Only one pass was needed. The two copters departed even before the flaming debris they'd caused had fallen to the ground.

In all, less than three minutes had elapsed since XBat had hit the ground. Whether all of the gunmen in the area had been killed or simply bowled over by the sudden violence of XBat's response, there was another lull in the incoming gunfire.

And that meant it was time to go . . .

On Autry's order, XBat started moving north, toward the area where Weir's copter had gone down. The unit had no real intelligence where the CIA agent was, or even if he was still alive. But again that didn't make much difference. If there was one thing XBat had excelled in during its short life, it was loyalty. To their country. To its citizens. To themselves. When someone was in trouble, XBat was on the scene. If someone needed rescuing, XBat was in the fore.

No one was ever left behind.

The soldiers started running along a side street off Bradley, moving quickly from doorway to doorway, their guns pointing in every direction, ready to fire if again fired upon. It was a nerve-wracking maneuver, a constant overlapping of security lines, checking every doorway, every abandoned car, anyplace someone could be hiding with an AK-47. Mogadishu or Fallujah hadn't been any worse than this.

Within seconds, though, they turned a corner and found themselves on the edge of MGM Square. This was where Weir's copter had gone down.

The square was across a wide street from the clutch of buildings where they thought the CIA agent's copter had crashed. As Autry's soldiers crept forward, most of XBat's copters were screaming overhead, their sound dampeners turned off, their engines bellowing, causing a deafening roar that was scary enough in itself. The idea was to unnerve any gunmen hiding around the square. Indeed, the noise was so loud, XBat had to communicate purely by hand signals.

Autry gazed out on MGM Square. There were several burning vehicles blocking their full view of the buildings on the other side. The streets to the north and south were filled with protesters in the midst of trashing businesses, so they weren't paying much attention at the moment.

The square itself was a large open area—and at the moment that was a big minus for XBat. Running to the buildings in question would be like running the length of a football field, exposed to fire from every direction. The alternative was no alternative at all, though: to move along the edges of the potential killing ground would take XBat valuable time, at least twenty minutes, if everything went smoothly. The burning cars had prevented the XBat copters from just landing here in the first place—but there was no use bitching about that now.

They knew they had no other choice. If they had any chance at all of locating Weir, they would have to make their way across the free fire zone and hope for the best.

That's why Autry decided that he would lead the charge himself.

He called up to one of the Flying Eggs, the closest copter to his position at the moment. Anticipating that their brethren on the ground would have to dash across this open area, the Egg pilots had been searching the rooftops and the alleyways for any possible positions gunmen might be hiding in. They couldn't see any—but that didn't mean gunmen weren't laying for them. There were many places that the copter pilots could *not* see; in fact, the smoke drifting over downtown was so thick by now, they barely had half the square in sight. The Egg pilots relayed these cold facts to Autry then assured him that if they detected any hostile fire during XBat's risky maneuver, they and the other copters would start laying down covering fire.

Autry took all this in and let it percolate for about two seconds. He knew there was no reason for further delay. He called up his first team—roughly one-third of his men—and told them to prepare to zigzag their way across the square, into the smoke and the buildings hidden beyond. He cautioned them to stay on his tail and stop only at the most convenient means of cover—the dozens of wrecked but nonburning cars littering the square. The second and third teams—the men carrying the unit's heavier weapons—would cover their run and then quickly follow.

Autry checked the clip in his special M-16 and took a deep breath. Earlier this morning he'd woken up in the desert with nothing more on his mind but how to kick ass on Zulu Force again. Now, it wasn't even noon yet, and he was suddenly in the middle of . . . what? The Second American Civil War? World War Three? He didn't know, and at the moment he didn't want to know.

One more breath, then he jumped up and started running.

It was strange, because he was instantly aware of the sound of his boots hitting the wet and oily pavement; at that moment it might have been the loneliest sound he'd ever heard. But then, an instant later, he heard more boots hitting the asphalt, followed by more and more—until it sounded like a stampede going across MGM Square. It made him warm inside—a weird sensation in this bit of heightened danger. But he knew all that noise meant he wasn't out here alone. His men were with him. In fact, they were right behind him.

He blared out orders while he ran, and on Autry's request one of the DAP Black Hawks swooped over the area. Its turbines absolutely screaming, again it made it impossible to hear anything else. But by coming down so low and so fast, it dispersed a major portion of the smoke that had been covering the north end of MGM Square, where the target buildings were.

Once this smoke screen parted, it became clear that the building directly ahead of them was a bank. Its windows were blown out, smoke was coming from the upper floors. Most unnerving, though, it was absolutely filled with armed men. Nearly the exact the description provided by the stranger on Weir's cell phone.

It was also clear that the people holed up inside the

bank weren't snot-nose rich kids with heavy weapons. These people, dozens of them, were all wearing black ski masks and red kerchiefs hiding their faces. They looked more like terrorists than simple anarchists. And by now they'd seen XBat coming.

Strangely, the cloud of thick smoke just as quickly obscured the two potential adversaries; the masked demonstrators and the hard-charging soldiers only saw each other for a few seconds. But that was enough. No sooner had the smoke moved back into place, hiding the building and its occupants again, than tracer fire started spitting out of the cloud and pinging all over the abandoned cars in the square.

Autry screamed an order and XBat's first team quickly dashed for cover among the wrecked cars. His men had their weapons up and aimed—they all had their IR scopes turned on too, and while not perfect, they did have some benefit in looking through smoke. Every trooper saw the same thing: a crowd of masked demonstrators inside the burned-out bank, staring out through the smoke, firing blindly.

There were also able to see what kind of weapons these people were armed with—and that too was disturbing. Not just AK-47s, but also RPG launchers. Autry's heart sank even further. A small army of heavily armed people had actually made it on to American soil and were now doing serious damage to the country's second largest city as well as the American psyche. It seemed unbelievable.

So much for Homeland Security.

Once all his men were under cover, Autry cried out another order: "Full combat array!" This was a slightly obscure way of saying: "Lock and load, and get ready to fight."

No sooner were the words out of his mouth than the barrage coming from the building intensified a hundred-fold. The tidal wave of AK-47 tracers was joined by streams of rocket propelled grenades whooshing over the heads of the special ops troopers and impacting on the previously trashed buildings beyond. Many of the XBat guys were veterans of a similar battle during the unit's North Korean adventure. They knew just how much damage a typical car could take from gunfire and rockets—and it was substantial. But not endless.

Still, the savvy troopers also knew that the more sustained the enemy's barrage, the quicker it would die away. And that's when XBat would once again bring its superior firepower to bear.

As predicted, the fusillade from the bank building died down in a few seconds, fading with a whimper. Many RPGs had been expended, and the buildings across the square had paid the price. But now the XBat troopers looked at each other and waited.

Finally, Autry bellowed two more words: *"Open fire!"*

GARY WEIR SAW IT COMING.

He was still propped up against the wall of the vault,

slumped in such a way that he could see right through the small bank, through the blown-away teller's stations, and out to the street. He too had a glimpse of this small army that had suddenly materialized on the other side of MGM Square. Through his bleary eyes, and barely conscious from his loss of blood, he thought this had to be a very large, reconstituted and emboldened LAPD SWAT team trying to attack the place.

In any case, they were now hidden by the smoke that had momentarily parted to reveal them, and when the huge barrage from the masked protesters followed, Weir was convinced by its ferocity that the L.A. SWAT guys would have to pull back and rethink their frontal assault.

This was both bad news and even worse news for him. Bad news because he knew if the police decided to simply freeze in place and wait it out, he would die, because he was smart enough to know that in his present condition he couldn't hold on much longer.

But the worse news was, if the cops kept on coming, the gunfire exchange would be so brutal, he probably would wind up dead anyway—from the friendly fire.

And that was one way he *didn't* want to go . . .

That's why he was so surprised when, in the next second, it seemed the world itself blew apart. He saw just a bright white light at first. Then the sound came—and then the fire and smoke. The white light turned red and orange and yellow all at the same time. Then the building itself started shaking around him.

This was enough to jolt Weir back into an upright sitting position. What was happening? Had one of the masked men's bombs gone off? Had something hit their ammunition supply?

His last guess was that the LAPD had continued their attack on the building. But in the same moment, he knew this could not be the case. The ordnance flying around. The tracers. The rapidity of explosions. This wasn't a police or SWAT action.

This was a military assault.

Combat soldiers were attacking the building. And he was right in the middle of it—and could do nothing about it. At that moment he wished that he'd had just died out in the alley and been done with it.

As these grim thoughts were going through Weir's head, two of the masked men appeared in the doorway leading to the vault. Speaking gibberish through their heavy masks, the two started arguing about something. With just about the last bit of strength he could muster, Weir cocked his good ear in their direction and was horrified to hear enough of the garbled English to know the two masked men were arguing about the best way to kill him.

One was saying they should just shoot him, his usefulness was now gone—plus they had to make their escape. The other was saying that the situation outside the vault was desperate and that they would need every bullet they had. He pulled out a huge machetelike knife as proof. He wanted to hack Weir to death.

This surreal argument seemed to go on and on. Weir was paralyzed from head to toe by now. All the while, the explosions and eruptions of fire continued around him. The noise was excruciating, the flames blinding. He could see other masked men farther out in the office firing their weapons, some controlled, some blindly. There were so many tracers bouncing around it was hard to say exactly who was shooting who. But Weir could tell just by the noise alone that the building was being assaulted by pros, and that they were close to overrunning it. In fact, he spotted at least a couple dozen of the masked gunmen fleeing through a large hole in the rear of the bank.

But this only intensified the argument between his two executioners. Finally one raised his knife, the other raised his gun. Then both let out a victory *whoop!* For some inconceivable reason, they had decided to kill Weir both ways. They stepped into the doorway of the vault itself. Weir couldn't have begged for his life even if he'd wanted to. He was too weak to talk, too weak to move. He could only sit there, staring up at his soon-to-be killers and begin wondering, from that moment until eternity, who the hell they really were.

They both got closer to him. Death was just a second away. He let out one last defiant curse . . .

Then an incredible surge of gunfire. And high-pitched screams from outside the vault. And suddenly flames everywhere. The floor was moving like an earthquake had hit or a nuke had gone off. Weir opened his eyes and saw the two masked men still standing over him, but now they were looking down at gaping holes in their chests. For a heartbeat Weir thought he was dead and this was hell because he'd never seen anything quite so horrible. It was like a special effect from a bad movie. The two men just standing there, oozing shock and surprise—with two holes blown clean through them.

This only lasted a microsecond, though. Both toppled over, as Weir realized that he'd gained a few more seconds of precious life thanks to the people who were assaulting the building and apparently tearing up the masked men with their superior firepower and tactics. But then the entire building started shaking again, and this time it started collapsing for real. Weir was sure a major support beam or something had been hit and that the bank building was coming down on top of him.

So he would not be shot or stabbed after all on this, his last day. Rather, he was going to be crushed to death.

Finally he just lay back and decided to accept it. Tears returned to his eyes. The building dissolving all around him. The noise was deafening.

But . . . then he felt someone grab him around the wrist. Someone else was gently slapping his face. Somehow Weir was able to open his eyes, thinking that death wasn't so painful after all, when he realized he was still among the living and that two enormous soldiers in heavy body armor and futuristic battle helmets were standing over him.

One of them pushed the face mask up from his helmet and looked down at him.

The CIA agent couldn't believe it.

It was Bobby Autry.

"Take it easy, partner," Autry told him. "We've come to get you out."

IT TOOK TWO MINUTES TO PULL WEIR FROM THE rubble.

And rubble it was. XBat's assault on the building, coupled with damage it had received earlier, had caused nearly half of it to collapse. Coming down with a great crash, it killed at least a couple dozen of the armed men, those not lucky enough to flee XBat's latest demonstration of concentrated fire. It had been Weir's only good luck that the gunmen had put him in the bank's vault. It was the only protected place on the first floor.

But still, he was seriously injured—and the rescue attempt had not been undertaken with XBat's usual near silent, stealthy approach. Although they'd been on the ground less than five minutes, they'd caused a racket and drawn a lot of attention. In fact, one of the more surreal aspects to all this was that hundreds of people were still trapped in the office buildings around MGM Square. These people were looking out their windows, eye-witnessing everything below. People were even taking pictures of the action with their camera phones—and anyone who saw these photos, military expert or not, would know right away that these weren't regular soldiers running through the streets of downtown L.A. on this day of never ending chaos. These soldiers were wearing black uniforms, oversized helmets, and carrying huge weapons. Their helicopters either made noise or they didn't, they flew high and low and performed some seemingly impossible maneuvers. And splashed over just about everything—the soldiers' uniforms, the helicopters, even some of the weapons— was their emblem: the stars of the constellation Orion the Sky Hunter, with the huge X running through it. X-Battalion. The Sky Hunters. The most secret unit of the highly secret TF-160 Nightstalkers. So many people had seen them by now, they might have been starring in their own movie.

Four troopers doing some artful rubble walking finally lifted Weir out of the smoldering building. Reaching the street, four more soldiers had an inflatable stretcher already deployed. They strapped Weir into it, then, through frantic hand signals, called in one of the Black Hawk troop ships. The pilots expertly put the copter down on the devastated street and Weir was placed on board.

The copter was told take off, but the pilots were suddenly waving madly at Autry. The unit CO ran around the front of the aircraft—it was obvious the pilot wanted to talk to him.

Autry reached the pilot's side window and pulled it open.

"Take him to the nearest hospital that isn't overflowing!" Autry yelled over the noise to the young pilot, a guy named Lynch.

But Lynch was shaking his head—he didn't need to know where Weir had to go. Instead he had an urgent message for Autry. Ever since Autry and his troops had landed for the assault on the bank building, the command copter had been trying to get ahold of him. Something very strange was happening.

"They say they've spotted an A-10 coming in from the east," Lynch yelled out to Autry. "He's carrying a full array of weaponry and all of it appears armed."

Autry just stared back at the pilot. All the noise and confusion going on around him suddenly came to a stop.

"What did you just say?" he yelled back at him.

"An A-10 showing a lot of attack profile is incoming," Lynch told him, louder this time. "The guys in the command copter have been tracking him for ten minutes. He's only about a minute out right now, and he looks like he's going into a preattack turn."

Autry's head started spinning. There was no way this was an authorized Air Force A-10 coming in. There was no way the Air Force would send *any* planes over the city at the moment—not with the SAMs as thick as rain in Topanga.

Lynch continued relaying information he was getting through his headset from the guys in the command copter. "They say that all three airport traffic control stations are trying to raise this aircraft on radio . . . but the pilot is not responding. Hold on a moment . . . Now they're saying an A-10 went missing from some kind of training flight in Arizona about an hour ago . . . He's definitely unauthorized . . . They're scrambling jets out of San Diego to come up after him . . . trouble is, he's already here . . ."

Autry thought he was going to lose it right there. If this loaded-up A-10 was unauthorized, then somehow, some way, the pilot must be in league with the demonstrators. But how or why would an Air Force pilot throw in with the likes of the anti-WTO protesters?

Autry didn't have a clue and didn't have any time to come up with any. It would take at least ten minutes for any high-speed jets to fly up from San Diego to deal with the A-10. By then the A-10 pilot would be over the city and doing what he'd flown here to do. And that could only be one thing: bomb the WTO meeting center. As crazy as it sounded.

Maybe all this was just a diversion, Autry thought with a chill. Maybe we've all been duped.

"They want to know what to do, sir," Lynch was yelling out at him.

Autry switched back into gear. "Tell them . . ." he began. "Tell them to go into prevent defense formation six. Like it or not, we're the only people around who can stop this guy."

CHAPTER 18

LIEUTENANT DAVIS SMITH WAS A REAL MESS BY THE
time his A-10 reached the outskirts of Los Angeles.

He was about to do something vilely wrong, unpatri-
otic and treasonous—yet none of that had any impact
on him now. He'd tried to commit suicide back over the
Arizona mountains, several times, in fact. But he just
didn't have the guts to fly himself into the ground. Sur-
viving that, his brain twisting a bit further, he'd made a
headlong dash across the California desert border, flying so low he was catching tumbleweed between his tail
fins. This would have been stressful on a typical fighter
pilot, but it was a piece of cake for him. He was a test
pilot, after all. A major god. It was once his job to try
to *make* airplanes crash.

What was bothering him at the moment, though, was
just how far into Mexico he would be able to fly before
he had to ditch the airplane. He was hoping to get as
far south as Punta San Carlos on the Baja. It was wild

country down there and he knew he could hide out long enough to get to his eventual destination: the state of Durango in central Mexico. This area was known as a haven for rich people on the run. And now he was rich. They would never find him down there.

But the air had been particularly thick coming over from Arizona, or at least in his mind it was, and thick air meant more fuel consumption. As it was, Smith had only about thirty-two minutes of gas left. It was enough for him to do what he'd come here to do, then swing out over the ocean, get lost in the shitty weather and head south. Just how far south was the question. And if interceptors were sent after him, a distinct possibility in the post-9/11 world? Well, that's when his test piloting skills would really come in handy. He would throw himself so far into the storm, no one would dare to follow. If he was lucky, they might think he crashed at sea—and not look for him at all.

He was soon just thirty seconds from the center of L.A. Flying way down at fifty feet, he was weaving his way up and over the high hills and around obstructions like power lines and cell phone towers, frightening hundreds of people in his subsonic wake. His one live Hellfire was armed and ready to go. All his pre-launch parameters were set in stone. The missile's nose cone was hot and it was already seeking out the laser target that an unknown confederate was suppose to shine on Smith's target. This was all he knew about his objective, which was good because he didn't want to know whose day he was about to ruin. While he just assumed all this had something to do with the huge protests the city had been expecting, as far as he was concerned now, his target was simply a point on a GPS screen. If someone on the ground was able to direct a laser targeting beam on the building where the people paying him wanted the missile to go, then he would release the missile and it would find the target itself.

So, boiled down, he was really being paid $2 million to simply flip a switch. Not a problem at all. Maybe if he hadn't abused drugs and alcohol over the past few years he would have felt different, would have felt something for the people he was about to blow to pieces. But at that moment, inside his belly, all he felt was cold.

He streaked over the last of the hills and turned northwest toward downtown L.A. He called up his GPS screen on his fairly rudimentary flight panel, and saw the prepositioned arrow pointing right at his target. He pushed another button, which showed him the target through an infrared scope. Sure enough, there was a blotch of laser light illuminating a building next to a golf course and a bunch of rolling hills.

"Must be the place," he mused.

He was approaching a forest of skyscrapers—the business district of downtown L.A. His target was a few miles beyond this gaggle of buildings. For him to stick with his attack profile—that was, to stay as low as possible for as long as possible—he would have to weave his way through these tall buildings, confusing anyone who might have a radar lock on him. Once past this obstacle course, he would be just seconds away from launching the Hellfire. Simple as that.

If I am truly blessed, he thought, the secreted bag of money stuck firmly between his legs, I'll be eating *tostadas* by sundown.

He entered the forest of buildings, aware that the streets below were in total chaos. Even cruising along at 140 knots, he could see gangs of masked protesters running wild, setting fires, smashing up businesses and firing weapons at police. Again, none of this was his affair. The United States went down the drain a long time ago, and something like this—like Katrina, like the fuck-up in Iraq, like 9/11—was actually long overdue. All the more reason to take the money and run. From the looks of things below, even Mexico had more law and order than this place.

He began twisting and turning his way through the clutch of buildings. He knew his jet engines were screaming, but the noise seemed to have little effect on the rioters. Even though steering the gangly attack plane in and around the buildings was a chore—one not taken lightly for a typical Thud pilot—Smith was doing it with ease. The U.S. Air Force not only taught him to fly, they'd taught him damn well. He couldn't imagine anything preventing him from completing this, his first and probably last, mercenary mission.

That all changed when he whipped the A-10 around the fifty-two-story PG&E Building and found himself looking at a huge Chinook helicopter coming at him from the opposite direction.

Smith's split-second instincts took over. Before he even knew he was doing it, he pulled the A-10 up and over the oncoming helicopter, growling his way up to two hundred feet and nearly hitting the cell phone tower atop the building. It was a gut-crunching maneuver, but all that experience flying X-planes had suddenly saved his life.

Only when he was able to level off again did he realize what had just happened. He'd come within a hair's breath of smashing into the suicidal copter. Who the hell was flying that thing? Was it a law enforcement aircraft having something to do with the citywide riot below? If so, since when did the LAPD start flying military-style Chinooks?

He didn't know, and really didn't care. He was back down flying among the buildings in a flash, trying to recover some airspeed, glad to still be alive, and chalking up the near collision to a million to one shot.

That's when he went around the Sony Records Tower—and found another helicopter waiting for him.

This one was a Black Hawk, and it wasn't spoiling for a head-on collision. Instead, it was hugging the side of the Sony building, almost as if its pilots knew he was coming and were waiting for him.

Again, all this happened in the blink of an eye. Smith had just enough time to pull his wings back to level before he found himself streaking past the stationary helicopter, a little slower because of his encounter with the Chinook. In the corner of his eye he saw a flash, and at the same moment felt a half-dozen dull thuds shake his aircraft. It was only after he swerved once again and started looping around the Cooley Gas Building that he realized the helicopter had shot at him.

Suddenly Smith was paying attention again. What was going on here? He'd thought the first encounter with the Chinook had been wrong place, wrong time. But now, as his ride got a little rougher, he realized these two copters might have been out to get him, the first one slowing him down just enough so the second one could get a shot at him. And judging from how his plane was swaying so suddenly, he had to believe that at least six cannon shells had torn up his two rear stabilizers, slowing his airspeed even further. This was crazy. Shooting down a jet aircraft was a very hard thing for a helicopter to do. Yet whoever had pulled the trigger in the lurking Black Hawk had come damn close to doing just that.

Smith soldiered on, a little shaky now but still committed to his bomb run. He turned the next corner, at the Palisades Industrial Tower, and this time found not one, but two Black Hawks waiting for him. Like the first one, they were hovering at his altitude, hanging side by side. They opened up on him as soon as he went by.

There were many loud thuds and they'd come closer to the cockpit than the first Black Hawk had. The A-

10 was rugged, built to take a lot of punishment above the battlefield and keep on flying. But he'd just taken a dozen more high-caliber cannon rounds to the fuselage—fired at almost point-blank range. How rugged could the plane be?

Again on instinct he pulled back on the controls and began to climb. But up at four hundred feet he found another nasty surprise: another Chinook, crossing paths with him as he slowed to turn again. The big copter actually kept pace with him for a moment, and in that time, at least a dozen weapons of all sizes and calibers opened up on him. It seemed incredible. Soldiers at the open cargo bays of the copter were shooting at him, just when he and his airplane were at their most vulnerable.

Smith dove again, intent on getting away from the skyscrapers and their hiding places. It was clear now: Not only were these copters out to get him, they had led him right into an ambush. No surprise then when he arrived back down to 150 feet and found yet another copter waiting for him. But this time he didn't fall for it. He twisted away long before anyone on the copter could take a shot at him—at least with a gun or cannon.

However, as he turned the bottom of his aircraft toward the copter, something unexpected happened—the copter fired a missile at him. It was not an antiaircraft missile, but it was a missile just the same, and in his foolishness he realized he had steered himself right into its flight path. This was nuts. It was as if the copters had anticipated exactly what he was going to do—like they had an eye in the sky or something—and then were exploiting it. He pushed his flare dispenser panel and a long string of flares began shooting out of the Thud's underbelly. He had to get away from this thing.

The countermeasure worked—just not quick enough. The flares caused the missile to explode prematurely, yet only twenty feet away from his cockpit.

The shock wave hit him like a truck. It was surprisingly powerful—what kind of missile was that? The A-10 nearly went over on its back. Smith had to call on all his experience just to keep level and out of a stall.

That's when his flight panel started screaming with warnings. He had many damaged systems, and many more systems that were in danger of failing completely. It looked like a Christmas tree, so many colored lights were blinking at him. Between the cannon hits and the missile's exploding warhead, the A-10 was suddenly full of holes.

"*Who the fuck are these guys?*" Smith bellowed. Again, helicopters weren't supposed to be able to shoot down jet aircraft, and certainly not without using antiaircraft weapons, which few copters carried. What copter pilot would take on an attack jet?

Finally Smith was aware enough to take significant action. As crazy or lucky or skilled as these mysterious copter pilots might be, there was one advantage he had over them: speed. He pushed his throttles ahead and rocketed away from the forest of skyscrapers.

But even as he did, he saw two more Black Hawks

trying to cut him off just as he was turning sharply over Venice Beach. They too fired missiles at him, from long range, but he released another string of flares and kept into the turn, essentially performing a 180 and facing his jet eastward, the one direction he did not want to go.

And sure enough, *another* pair of copters was waiting about 3,000 feet ahead of him. They too fired missiles and sent a few cannon shots his way. Smith maneuvered easily away from this combined barrage and in that instant realized that while the copters had done their best to stop him, they had failed, as he was now flying faster than any copter could go. And just by his good luck, his target area was right in front of him.

His aircraft finally stabilized itself. A lot of the A-10's redundant systems had kicked in and the plane was flying OK for the time being. He looked down at his weapons panel and saw that not only was his Hellfire missile still hot, it had acquired a definite lock from the laser targeting device being reflected off the target just two miles ahead. He put his finger over the Missile Fire button.

"Now comes the easy part," he said with a dark grin.

MADNESS...

That was the only word bouncing around Bobby Autry's head at the moment. He was flying his DAP ship again, moving his hands and feet in the way that they should move to keep the Black Hawk in the air—but in truth, he wasn't paying attention. The copter was flying itself. He'd seen too much, done too much this disturbing morning, to be thinking clearly anymore. The loss of five of his guys. The brutal revenge attack on the defenseless first freighter. The bloody rescue of Agent Weir, the carnage and destruction XBat had left behind. It was like a nightmare that just wouldn't stop. No matter what he and the team did, something even more evil or dangerous always cropped up.

This was so true of this rogue A-10. It was here, though it shouldn't be. The rioting going on below. The destruction of L.A. The inevitable repercussions of this to the American way of life. None of it should have been happening, but it was.

Madness . . .

With all time stopped, and only these crazy thoughts running through his head, it was becoming clear to Autry that the running gun battles below were just a planned distraction. A distraction for what was happening in front of him. His proof: No SAMs had been fired at the A-10 as it passed over the riot-strewn city. While everyone was looking for threats on the ground, someone had arranged for this A-10 to fly in, throw a missile into the building where the President and the WTO leaders were meeting, using, Autry guessed correctly, someone else on the ground at the resort to illuminate the target with a laser designator. What would be the result of this? A mass assassination. In one explosion, cutting off the heads of government of the ten most powerful countries in the world. Global chaos could only ensue.

XBat had tried its best to stop the A-10. They'd mastered the odd art of dogfighting amidst skyscrapers during their last mission in Venezuela. It was all about setting up a string of ambushes, enough to confuse the pilot into going this way instead of that, as well as calling on the quirky G-Net to predict the A-10's every move.

It had almost worked. The only problem was that the jet was too fast and the copters just a bit too lightly armed to bring down the flying tank. And now, even as Autry watched, the A-10 streaked away, going into its final turn to commence its attack on Briar Patch. And there was nothing he could do about it except watch the A-10 fade from his G-Net readout screen. Even trying to get a message to Briar Patch was too little, too late, though Autry's radioman was giving it a try.

That's why what happened next was so strange.

If Autry hadn't seen it with his own eyes, he would have never believed it was true. But just as the A-10 began its final attack run, a bolt of blue lightning suddenly appeared in the sky and, with a thunderous report, struck the A-10 right at mid-fuselage. The airplane simply disintegrated. No fire, no smoke, hardly any debris. It had been obliterated.

"What happened?" Zucker cried out.

Autry was stunned—but for some reason his eyes went from the puff of sickly red hanging in the air in front of him to his G-Net readout screen. The screen was blinking furiously and displaying a loop that showed with no uncertainty that the G-Net had emitted some kind of electronic bolt that had come down from the heavens and vaporized the rogue A-10.

"Jesus Christ," Autry breathed. "It *is* a weapon . . ."

The crew in his copter cheered the near miraculous event. But then came the bad news—directly from McCune's command chopper. Yes, he confirmed that the Galaxy Net had knocked the A-10 out of the sky. However, the pilot had already fired his Hellfire missile before the A-10 was destroyed. The Hellfire was now gliding on a course set for it by the laser beam being reflected off the side of the resort's meeting hall. Its warhead was active. It would hit its target in less than thirty seconds.

Zucker just looked over at Autry, stunned at this, the weirdest turn of all. "This just isn't our day," he said.

But Autry suddenly had his radio mic turned on.

"Maybe," he said. "But maybe not."

MUNGO WASN'T SUPPOSED TO BE ANYWHERE NEAR Briar Patch in the seconds after the A-10 launched its missile.

He was flying one of the Killer Eggs, alone, as usual. He too was still soaking wet after trying to swim across the channel from the islands to the mainland. He'd served as a kind of down-and-dirty scout for the Weir rescue mission, making continuous dives on large bands of protesters who'd been attracted by the noise of XBat's sudden arrival in MGM Square.

He kept these onlookers at bay while the XBat ground troops did their thing. As soon as the rest of XBat was pulled out, Mungo left as well, suddenly freeing a torrent of protesters who were now able to run wild in the square and see the destruction that XBat had just wrought.

But once Weir was free, Mungo headed right for Briar Patch, thinking this was where the rest of the unit would naturally go next. Exactly why he missed all the radio calls alerting the team that they had to try to stop the rogue A-10—well, that would never really be known.

All that was for sure was that when he arrived over the exclusive resort, he saw chaos on the ground, two presidential helicopters burning, large crowds of protesters heading toward the place from all directions— and not a cop in sight.

He had one more surprise coming too. He turned his small copter into a 180, and instead of seeing the rest of XBat right on his heels, found instead that he was flying above the resort alone.

What happened next would be talked about for years to come. Hundreds of people would claim that they were there and that they saw it, but actually there were only about a dozen eyewitnesses. The retellings would contain some distortions too, understandable for history-changing events that bordered on legend.

The first distortion was the Mungo actually saw the Hellfire missile coming. This was not true. He never had any angle that would have given him a field of view to pick up the missile until the very last moment.

What actually happened was that Autry called Mungo and gave him a simple order: "Laser-initiated weapons retrack."

It was one of many plays in XBat's playbook. Mungo remembered it exactly.

He didn't even think about it. He simply turned on the Killer Egg's S2A—its surface surveillance array. This provided him with an infrared view of the ground, with the emphasis on looking for any kind of radiation being emitted from a weapon, or something attached to a weapon. With one flick of a switch, Mungo saw a long red line coming out of the corner room of the building next to the resort's meeting hall and splashing itself against the glass of the huge flying-saucer-shaped room.

Mungo knew right away this was a laser target designator. So he had found the so-called "laser-initiated weapons" part of his order. Now, he had the "retrack" part to do.

The Killer Egg had its own laser targeting system; all the copters in XBat did. He quickly swooped down and pointed his laser beam right at the source of the long red beam. Mungo's laser was more powerful, it was simple as that. He held the beam steady, to the point where he actually saw someone in the corner room pull back the drapes and look right at him. This man, the would-be assassin, knew what was going on. He also knew what was going to happen next. Legend said he actually saluted Mungo.

The Hellfire appeared over the resort a moment later and started falling toward the flying saucer meeting hall. But just an instant before it slammed into the all-glass structure, it locked onto Mungo's stronger laser beam. It did an about face—and slammed into the corner room instead.

There was a frightening explosion. A fireball leaped into the air, causing another wave of dark smoke to envelop the area. When the smoke cleared, it showed the corner room had been obliterated, along with half of the resort's otherwise empty wing.

That's when Mungo coolly cued his chin mic and reported back to Autry: "Incoming weapon has been 'retracked' . . . Any further orders?"

Briar Patch

Though it missed killing everyone inside the meeting hall, the Hellfire missile nevertheless shook the flying-saucer-shaped building to its foundation.

Several of the large, weirdly curved panes of glass came crashing to the floor. Sparks spewed from the room's ultra-high-tech TV screen and communication suite. Fire alarms throughout the resort were activated by the blast. Klaxons started blaring, and the sprinkler system inside the meeting room turned itself on, showering those below with a spray of tepid water.

The Secret Service agents immediately began yelling: "Get him out! Get the President out!" But it was no use. Both presidential helicopters had been destroyed and there wasn't another helicopter for miles secure enough to carry the POTUS out.

The situation quickly became worse. No sooner had the smoke cleared from the Hellfire blast when Fred Haas, the lead Secret Service agent, received a devastating report: Hundreds of anti-WTO protesters had converged on both the north and south gates of the resort. Having broken through on two fronts, near Wilshire Avenue and, unexpectedly, coming down Topanga Way, out of the hills to the east, these people had been completely overlooked by authorities. Those LAPD officers who'd stayed behind to protect the resort clashed with the vanguard of this third wave of protesters, then either ran away or were overrun. Like their colleagues downtown, they were underequipped and outnumbered. They were no match for the heavily armed protesters. The same was true for many of the resort's own private security force. They too had vanished after a few brief skirmishes with rampaging demonstrators.

Although the building right next door was aflame, the President and the other dignitaries were still contained in the saucer-shaped meeting hall—wet, uncomfortable, but at least still alive. Despite missing a few of its expensive glass panes, it had been deemed the most secure place on the sprawling resort. At least for the moment.

Haas and his men began examining their next option, which was a desperate land exit. It would be tricky. The six SUVs still in drivable condition at the resort were Grade 6 security, meaning they were heavily armored, bulletproof glass, steel tires—as reinforced as the President's limousine. But with both main entrances now blocked by the protesters, the only option was to clear a hole in the resort's outer fence and drive out that way. It would be undignified, to be sure—but that was just the beginning of the problem. Once they were out of the resort, where could they go? LAX was twenty-two miles away. There were several small airports in the area where a secure helicopter could land, if one could be found. Another alternative would be to head for the sizable CHP barracks about a mile and a half mile away. A copter could also land there.

But no matter what option they chose, the SUVs would still have to plow through a sea of protesters. To be mowing down these people, especially if they were not armed, would be a moment they would gladly avoid. But the Secret Service had no choice. There was no other way out.

Haas had spent the last ten minutes just a half step away from the POTUS, his body being the Chief Executive's last line of defense before disaster. He had informed the President that they were "egressing via a land route" and that, once again, they were planning to leave immediately. The POTUS looked more than anxious to leave the area.

They began walking through the glass-shattered remains of the flying saucer building. But then came the call Haas had really been dreading: A report on what was going on just outside the resort said the protesters had commandeered several large trucks, had driven them close to the resort, turned them over and set them ablaze. They were now blocking the two main access streets on either side of Briar Patch—the streets the Secret Service had planned on using in their land-egress option.

In other words, everyone inside the resort was trapped.

Haas forcibly turned the POTUS around and marched him back to the rear of the meeting room. The explosions started going off a moment later.

Leaving the Chief Executive with his inside team of agents, Haas ran back to the meeting hall's door. From there he saw plumes of flames and smoke erupting down near the seventh hole, about five hundred yards from the meeting room itself. The fiery flashes cut through the substantial banks of smoke enveloping the area. They were accompanied by sharp reports, indicating they contained ordnance as opposed to any kind of high explosive. Crude antipersonnel bombs? Haas wondered. Or were they just flares?

This rain of fire had Haas and his two senior men discussing their final option: essentially getting the President to the most secure place on-site and forming a protective ring around him. At the same time they were still frantically calling for any helicopters in the area to come to Briar Patch; they were even trying to contact media copters—any kind of aircraft at all to lift the President out. But no copter pilot dared fly anywhere near Beverly Hills for fear of getting shot down.

Haas quickly determined that a small office located in the basement of the main resort was the safest place in a pinch. But just as he was about to begin herding the President and the other dignitaries to this space, he heard more explosions—and these weren't out on the fairway. They were landing on top of the saucer building itself. And judging by the accompanying shock waves, they were definitely not flares.

The normally cool Secret Service guys started to sweat now, Haas included. It wasn't that their normal security procedures hadn't worked. A near comedy of errors and circumstances had befallen them, with every turn of events going against them. It was almost as if they were fated to lose today, bright stars turned cold.

Looking back out of the meeting room's shattered windows, Haas saw the most alarming sight of all. Not only were explosions going off all around them, the fairway was now filled with protesters. Coming out of the smoke and fog like some kind of disorganized ghost army, some were running, some were walking. Those out front were charging up the hill right near the saucer building. Many were armed and seemed determined to get into the meeting hall. And there were hundreds of them—against Haas and his dozen Secret Service agents.

Haas grabbed eight of his agents and rushed back outside. They immediately formed a firing line. They were armed with automatic rifles, a few with tear-gas dispensers attached. Each agent was also carrying a Beretta nine-shot pistol, plus a personal weapon, usually a .38 special.

With this amount of firepower, Haas knew he and his men could probably take down about a hundred of the protesters before their ammo ran out or they were killed themselves. Trouble was, there were at least five hundred protesters heading right for them.

"How did it ever come to this?" Haas wondered aloud.

But then, a miracle. Or something close to one.

It seemed at first like the sky was falling in. The overcast got darker even as the black smoke drifting over the resort suddenly cleared away. Then came the noise, the scream of eleven combat assault helicopters all descending at once. More dust blowing, more smoke swirling about. The symphony of engines and rotors overwhelmed all other noise resulting from the chaos. It took just a few seconds for all eleven aircraft to touch down.

X-Battalion had landed.

As Haas and his men retreated, intent on keeping

everyone inside the meeting hall, soldiers jumping out of the helicopters rushed forward to form another, much larger line separating the resort from the advancing protesters. The smoke returned with a vengeance, obscuring the soldiers' movements from being seen by the demonstrators on the fairway below. Still, the small army continued to march up the hill. No longer the chaotic rabble, it seemed like the several hundred protesters had coalesced into a fairly unified front.

Once they were close enough, though, the smoke cleared again and what the approaching protesters saw gave them pause. Three lines of soldiers were facing them. The first line was in a flat-out prone position. The second line were in a crouch. Behind them, the third line of soldiers was standing. It looked like a massive firing squad. Each soldier was pointing his weapon directly at the mass of demonstrators. Each weapon had its laser sighting device turned on, causing thirty-six distinct streaks of red light to penetrate the smoke and fog that still separated the two opposing forces.

The wave of demonstrators slowed at the sight of the black camo phalanx. Confusion rippled through their ranks. It was three dozen heavily armed soldiers against the five hundred or so demonstrators, some armed, but some not. What would be the outcome of this? Somewhere behind the scenes Agent Haas was shouting through a bullhorn, ordering the protesters to disperse. But no one was listening to him. Just one hundred feet away now, they kept coming, albeit very slowly.

Autry was the last soldier in the third line. He had his weapon up and aimed and ready to fire. But his hands were shaking badly, a problem for everyone in XBat. None of them wanted to be here, none of them wanted to do this. But it was their job. Trouble was, it would be Autry's call whether to open fire on the mob or not.

Kent State . . .

Those two words were going through Autry's head. May 1970. National Guard troops fired on students protesting the Vietnam War, killing four. Of course, those protesters weren't carrying weapons. But still, America was never the same after that.

So, what would happen, Autry thought, after *this?*

He looked into the crowd, at their eyes and their hands. Maybe every tenth person was wearing both a ski mask and red kerchief, just like the people they'd seen back at the burned-out bank—in fact these might have been the very people who'd escaped from the collapsed building. It was now obvious they were the hardcore, thug-types probably linked with the mystery guy who'd nearly vaporized the President with a Hellfire missile minutes before.

But it was the other faces that were burning onto Autry's retinas now, the other ninety percent of the mob. Most of them really *were* just kids. And yes, some were carrying baseball bats, but many were unarmed. In their eyes, Autry saw pure confusion. This was the worst of all possible scenarios: the hard-core people using the dedicated but not necessarily murderous protesters as a shield. And maybe *that* had been the plan all along.

The line of demonstrators finally came to a stop about fifty feet from the XBat troopers. A whiff of tense indecision went through the air. The protesters had made it this far—crazily enough, their ultimate goal of busting into the resort had been achieved. But it was as if no one knew what to do next.

Several seconds passed . . . Autry and his men did not move an inch. This was as much about appearances and visuals as it was about how much firepower so many soldiers with so many machine guns could put into a mostly unarmed crowd. And Autry prayed. For the first time since he was a little kid he prayed that somehow, some way, some divine intervention would arrive, like a bolt from the blue, courtesy of the Galaxy Net, to infuse some sanity into the situation. These kids, the ones without the guns. *Please,* he thought over and over, *just make them all turn around and go home.*

But it was not to be.

Because one man, in a mask and kerchief, lurking behind the first line of protesters, stuck his gun through their ranks. It was Jerome. He pulled his trigger and a single bullet hit one of the Chinook pilots on the third line, a WSO named Fogarty. Luckily, he was wearing his bulletproof battle vest—and the bullet literally bounced off. But that didn't make any difference. As soon as Autry realized what had happened, he had no choice.

He gave the order for XBat to open fire.

And no sooner were the words out of his mouth when Bobby Autry heard three strange noises come from deep within his head.

Not pounding. Not echoing. And not the sound of a bullet going through his skull. At least he didn't think so.

No—coming from that part of his brain where his very sanity lay, the three noises sounded almost familiar.

They went *snap, crackle* and *pop* . . .

IT WAS ALL OVER IN LESS THAN THIRTY SECONDS.

The fusillade delivered by XBat hit the protesters like a battering ram. It rolled over them, cutting many in two, mowing others down like a scythe.

It was loud, horrible and bloody. And much too quick for any of the hard-core gunmen in the crowd to return fire. Those few protesters lucky enough to escape the initial barrage were allowed to run away. Many threw down their baseball bats as they did so. No XBat trooper was hurt much more than Fogarty, who would have a sore shoulder for a while.

But when the smoke finally cleared, 352 demonstrators lay dead.

THE WTO LEADERS WERE QUICKLY BROUGHT OUT to the huge parking lot. The danger was not over, not exactly anyway. But they were going to be evacuated at last, by XBat.

The dignitaries were unceremoniously lifted aboard the helicopters, including the POTUS, who was placed aboard McCune's command Chinook and strapped into the jump seat right behind the pilot's station. Soaking wet, face ashen, eyes swollen, the Chief Executive looked absolutely mortified.

Far from being in awe, the XBat troopers on the command copter were tired, dirty, and disgusted at what had just happened. They were also very pissed off at what they'd gone through in the past twenty-four hours. They'd been dragged into a small war playing out on American streets, with this pish-posh piece of crap country club being Ground Zero.

They couldn't wait to get the hell out of there.

Being a politician, the POTUS wasn't really a strong man. It just wasn't in his genes. His humiliation quickly bubbled over into rage, though, and he was suddenly swearing a blue streak. Talking over everyone else, he was screaming at his aides: How could they let this happen? How could these punks have been able to pull this off? How were they able to suck in so many thousands of people to help them embarrass the administration?

For some reason he was screaming most of this directly into McCune's ear. As if him being the pilot of the copter made him the most likely target to attack. Over and over the Chief Executive kept saying, "Where were my advisors? Where was all my advice?"

Finally McCune could take it no more. He turned around in his seat and said directly to the President, "Want some advice? Next time you're supposed to be talking about hunger and poverty around the world, maybe do it someplace other than in the middle of Beverly Hills . . ."

Suddenly there was no sound. Everyone on board the copter was shocked.

Then McCune added, "Now keep your mouth shut and let me fly this aircraft."

And *that* was the end of XBat.

CHAPTER 19

BOBBY AUTRY SPENT THE NEXT FEW WEEKS IN A PRI-
vate hospital somewhere near San Diego.

He was put in a sealed-off room and attended to
by Navy doctors only. He didn't have any serious
injuries—or at least that's what he was told. Rather,
he'd suffered just a few small physical wounds at the
Massacre at Briar Patch, as it came to be called: shrap-
nel in his arm, a burn to his thigh, a bullet fragment
in his head.

The Navy doctors never let on whether they knew
how he'd gotten banged up; they'd mentioned how
they'd treated more than a few SEALs at their facility over the years, and none of them had arrived in
any worse shape than Autry. But when Autry asked if
any SEALs were there now—or if the hospital had any
other patients at all—the doctors always changed the
subject.

This was also true when Autry asked about the guys

in XBat. It seemed like forever since he'd been in touch with the team. But other than telling him that everyone who'd been present at Briar Patch had made it through alive, the doctors never offered anything more.

Most of the time Autry just slept. He watched no TV, and never looked at any of the newspapers the doctors brought to him. In the first few days of his stay, he'd expected the door to open at any moment and some dick from the NSC to walk in and give him the worst third-degree grilling imaginable. But it never happened. No one came to visit him. And the doctors never mentioned anyone even trying.

Until his last day.

It began when a man in very plain civilian clothes strolled into his room. Autry didn't recognize him at first. Barrel-chested, stout, bald—it was Major Jim Shaw. In the twenty-five years Autry had known him, this was the first time he'd seen him *not* wearing his uniform.

Shaw shook Autry's hand. "The Angel of Death has arrived," he said with a smile.

Autry smiled back, even though it felt strange. One of Shaw's many duties in his years at the Pentagon was delivering orders for high-ranking special ops guys, veterans of highly classified operations. While these orders could hold promotions or plum assignments, Shaw's visits usually entailed him handing over a letter informing the officer that he'd been passed over for promotion—and that usually meant a death sentence.

And indeed, this day, what Shaw had to tell Autry was life changing.

"People you both know and don't know went to bat for you in Washington," Shaw explained to him. "You and your men. They appreciate the circumstances you faced. They recognize your bravery. And they are grateful for it. That's why they're letting you out of here."

Autry felt a great weight lift off his shoulders, even though he had no idea what he was going to do when he took that first step out of the hospital. He shook Shaw's hand again for a long time, his relief evident.

"But truly," Shaw told him, "they want you to lay as low as you can, forever—and don't ever tell anyone anything about the unit and what happened on your missions. OK?"

Autry smiled again. "Who the hell am *I* going to tell?" he said. "No one would believe me."

AUTRY SIGNED HIMSELF OUT AND SHAW WALKED with him to the street. A government-issue car was waiting in front of the hospital. Two obvious undercover guys were riding up front.

Shaw directed Autry toward it.

"Thought you'd like to see a couple of sights before you shipped out," he said cryptically.

Autry just shrugged and climbed into the back of the car. It quickly sped away.

They drove along the waterfront. The ride was pleasant enough. Autry couldn't remember the last time he'd gone for a simple drive. It was bright and sunny and he actually felt oddly relaxed. Of course, he was full of painkillers and other medications he believed added to this feeling of well-being.

The car finally stopped in front of an old armory. Located on the outskirts of a small coastal town, the sign out front said it was the home of the 5678th Military Police Battalion of the California National Guard. Shaw led Autry inside. Walking through the door was like walking into a refrigerator. It was freezing!

Shaw flashed his ID card to the small army of plainclothes security men guarding the main door. Allowing them inside, he and Autry had to pass several more checkpoints before they got to their destination, which was the armory's main assembly hall. It was a huge place; it seemed way too big to fit inside the old red brick building. It was also sectioned off with thin cubiclelike walls seen more readily in emergency rooms and trauma centers. And it was so cold inside, Autry could see the condensation in his breath.

"What do you have in here?" Autry asked. "Alien bodies?"

"Close enough," Shaw replied mysteriously.

They walked into an enclosed cubicle next to the main entrance. It smelled heavily of embalming fluid and ether. In the middle of the room was a stainless steel table holding a body covered with a sheet.

Shaw unceremoniously pulled the covering away. The body beneath was badly injured and burned.

"This was the guy who snuck into the resort," Shaw explained plainly. "He brought the laser targeting device with him. He somehow got hooked up with the A-10 driver, who was up to his eyeballs in gambling debt and had a bunch of leg-breakers after him—so we know he went along with it for the money. This guy's job was to flash the laser on the building where the President was, and let the A-10's Hellfire missile do the rest. As it turned out, the missile went right down his own throat. This is what happens to you when a Hellfire blows up your ass."

But Autry was only half listening. He was looking at the dead man's face instead. Though it was grotesquely distorted, he recognized its features.

He was astonished. He actually knew this person.

"It's that guy Bolick, *Douglas Bolick*, from the New York CIA station," Autry said. "He used to work with Weir's group. He was the first CIA type to put together the North Korean problem."

Shaw nodded in agreement. "Yeah—I knew him too."

Autry's head began to spin, a very uncomfortable proposition these days. Bolick was a loyal government agent who helped save the world back when the U.S. first found out that North Korea had a Doomsday Weapon. Why would *he* try to kill the President?

Shaw read his mind.

"He left a note," he told Autry. "He explained that he'd seen too many of his friends die due to the incompetence of this administration. People he'd been close to, in Iraq and Afghanistan, had been killed for no reason and it drove him nuts. He even quoted a passage from Thomas Jefferson in his note: 'Whenever any form of government becomes destructive to life, liberty, and the pursuit of happiness, it is the right of the people to alter or abolish it, and to institute new government.' "

Autry just shook his head. "Pretty heavy," he murmured.

"Mr. Bolick here didn't care much for the other WTO leaders either," Shaw concluded. "Those were the reasons he gave for trying to pull this off."

Shaw retrieved a sheet from the examining table file holder.

"His toxicology report also showed he was full of stuff like Ambien—that sleeping pill that causes blackouts? An antidepressant medication. On and on, a lot of this wacky stuff that is on the market these days. He had a lot of it running through him. All of it by prescription."

Autry looked up at Shaw. "But do you believe him?"

Shaw lowered his voice. "The reasons he gave for doing this, you mean?"

"Yes . . ." Autry replied. "Or was it a setup? After all, look who he worked for."

Shaw almost went pale. "Are you asking me if the CIA was behind this whole thing, the demonstrations, the arms shipment, as a plot to kill the POTUS?"

Autry straightened up. "For whatever reason, yes— that's exactly what I'm asking you."

Shaw just looked down at the body and shook his head.

"I don't know," he said, adding: "And, frankly, I don't *want* to know."

They left the icy cubicle and went through another checkpoint. Here, they passed several layers of the separators before finding themselves inside the big room itself.

This place was so cold, the frozen condensation on the floor, walls and ceiling looked like snow.

Spread out before them, lying on cots, were a couple hundred bodies.

These were the hard-core anti-WTO protesters killed during the day of hell in Los Angeles, Shaw explained. The guys wearing the ski masks *and* the red kerchiefs to hide their faces. Though covered with thin white sheets, it was obvious many were burned or mangled beyond recognition.

"Who were they?" Autry asked him somberly.

"No one knows," Shaw replied again with a shake of his head. "And no one has stepped forward to claim any of their bodies. That might be the strangest thing of all. You would have thought at least a few of these people would have families somewhere looking for them. But it has yet to be."

A *really* secret army? Autry wondered. Or a collection of highly trained, highly motivated misfits who had nothing better to do then turn the U.S. upside down? Or were they part of something entirely different? Either way, they'd brought Baghdad-type warfare to the streets of L.A., and the country would never be the same for it.

Shaw just shrugged again. "None of these people were carrying ID. We don't know if they arrived mixed in with the rest of the WTO protesters, or from the cargo ship, or whether they all came from someplace else. It *was* planned, though, very thoroughly. That much we do know."

The Army major hesitated, then went on: "But *who* were they? I'm not sure it makes any difference. The Romans didn't take names when the barbarians showed up at their gates. Maybe these people are the sons of every little guy from every little country that the U.S. has screwed over the years. Or maybe they're from countries we've barged into, saying we know better than you about how to run your own lives. Or maybe they were all just hired thugs. But, when you think of it, who *cares* who they were? They're just bit players at the beginning of the end. The American Empire is beginning to fall. And we are here to see it."

Autry ran his hands over his dirty head. His bandages felt moist all of a sudden.

"Thanks for that bit of sunshine," he told Shaw glumly.

*   *   *

THE MORBID TOUR OVER, SHAW LED AUTRY BACK TO the front door of the armory.

They shook hands, and Autry suddenly felt a great friendship was coming to an end. The chances they'd ever see each other again were remote.

Autry began to go into a goodbye speech, but Shaw stopped him. "I've got one more thing to show you," he said.

He brought Autry outside to the armory parking lot. To his surprise there was a helicopter waiting here. A very civilian-looking Bell.

"This guy said he'd give you a lift," Shaw told Autry.

With that, Shaw disappeared forever.

Autry turned to the copter. The pilot was motioning to him. He walked over and opened the door. Behind the controls was Gary Weir.

He looked thinner, paler, and was still sporting a few wounds. But Autry was amazed to see him alive at all.

"I'm sure *this* is not authorized," Autry told him, looking around the helicopter's cockpit.

Weir just laughed. "What fun would that be?"

Autry climbed in. "Where are we going? Vegas?"

Weir laughed again. "Just sit back and chill. There's someplace else you've got to go."

Autry took his advice. With the painkillers still making their way through his system, he felt mellower than usual. Plus, he hadn't been airborne in a while. Any opportunity he had to fly these days, he had to grab it while he could.

They lifted off, went over the armory and turned north. Soon they were out over the California beaches. They seemed oddly clean, warm and inviting. The water was a very deep blue.

They flew along the coast for about a half hour. Finally, Weir started descending. He was heading for a small field near some rolling green hills, right near the water. Weir circled the field once then set down.

Autry looked over at him. "What is this?"

Weir reached over and shook his hand. "This is where you get off. Consider it a long-deserved R and R."

Autry climbed out, mystified. Weir gave him one last salute, which Autry returned, knowing he would probably never see Weir again either.

The copter took off and disappeared to the south, leaving Autry alone. He looked around the field of sand grass, wondering what was happening, or if anything was happening at all. Had he been on the pain medication too long? Or not long enough? And why was his head bandage always moist?

Time passed. A minute. An hour. He couldn't tell for sure. Finally, though, he saw a person approaching, walking down a path from one of the grassy hills. This person was calling his name. There was still a bit of morning mist left, so at first Autry couldn't make out who it was exactly.

But then a convenient wind came along and blew the fog away and Autry could see the person clearly.

He was shocked.

It was his wife.

And she was smiling.

THE COTTAGE WAS RIGHT ON THE BEACH. WITH SAND dunes on three sides to make it private, the ocean was a hundred feet from the back door.

This was where Autry's wife lived—and now he lived with her. She was taking care of him, feeding him meds and making sure his head bandage didn't get too moist.

He spent much of his time out on the back porch, rocking in his chair, looking at the ocean. Hours, days, weeks passed. It was hard to tell. His wife would sometimes come out and sit with him, sometimes they'd do therapy. And sometimes he would catch her wiping her eyes with a Kleenex. She would tell him it was because she was so happy they were together again. Never, though, did they talk about what happened at Briar Patch, or the order Autry had given before his head went *snap, crackle, pop.*

One day she showed him a picture, fuzzy and green, as if it had been taken through a NightScope lens. It appeared to show a container ship, with some kind of military activity going on around it. The ship's name was *Ocean Voyager.* And standing on the stern, along the handrail above the name, was Gary Weir. He seemed to be waving goodbye to Autry.

Another day she told him he'd received a letter from

his old friend, Captain Mungo. Autry studied the letter but couldn't read it. So his wife read it to him.

It was an explanation of why Mungo supposedly chickened out that day, in 1993, in Mogadishu, when he didn't go on the infamous "Black Hawk Down" mission. And apparently the rumors were true. It *was* all about a woman. Someone Mungo had met, somehow, in the wild back streets of the starving and bloody Somali capital.

His story was so sweet and heroic that Autry could almost hear violins as his wife read on. It was a tale right out of *Romeo and Juliet*. Love found, lost, found again—then tragedy. And after hearing it, Autry had a whole new appreciation for Mungo. He also realized he owed the junior officer a grand apology, and he would have tried to do that somehow, except that a few days later, when he asked his wife to read him the letter again, she told him, sweetly, that she didn't recall him getting any such letter.

ONE MORNING HE WOKE UP IN HIS ROCKING CHAIR TO hear someone knocking on the cottage's front door.

His wife came out to the porch soon afterward, smiling, happy, but wiping her teary eyes again. She told Autry he had a visitor. The next thing Autry knew, he was looking up at Sheriff Kemp. The guy who'd held him captive at the Grape River airfield.

"I am very glad to see you," Kemp told him, sitting

down in the rocking chair next to him. "And I want you to prepare yourself for a shock. I have three things to tell you, and it might be too much good news for you to handle all at once."

Autry just stared back at him. Too much good news? He wondered if there was really such a thing.

"Let me start with your guys," Kemp began. "Ozzo and his crew? The ones you thought had been shot down? Well, they're not dead. They were hit bad after they found the two freighters, but they managed to fly away. They crash-landed near an oil farm just outside the Port of L.A. The copter sank and they walked in mud for a half a day before being found."

But Autry was confused. "But I saw their chopper get obliterated," he said.

Kemp stuck his finger in the air. "Ah—but not really. You actually saw what the Galaxy Net *thought* it saw. It screwed up when it transmitted the clip to you. It was a virtual clip, but you saw it as if it was real. So, bottom line, your guys made it and are safe."

Autry suddenly choked up. His wife was standing behind him. She put her hand on his shoulder.

"Piece of good news number two," Kemp went on. "The Coast Guard cutter made it too. It's safe with all hands onboard. Again, the Galaxy Net screwed up. But not in the way everyone thought. The mooks *did* fire an antiship missile at it. But the range was actually too close. The missile exploded, wrecked their gears, but the ship never went down. It was tossed around out there for the next couple days, with no radios, no steering. But they finally managed to point their bow east and beach themselves down near Juarez. The Mexicans thought we were invading."

Autry's heart was beating hard now. No doubt about that. Two pieces of good news. One more to go.

"I bet I know what the third piece of good news is," he said excitedly. "That my unit isn't really broken up?"

But the visitor just dropped his head for a moment. Then he tapped Autry on the knee.

"No, sorry, Bobby—that part *is* true."

He reached inside his jacket pocket and came out with a yellow envelope. He handed it to Autry. "*This* is the third part of the good news."

Autry opened it. There was a million dollars in cash inside. But the bills were so new, they looked suspiciously like play money.

"You don't have to worry about anything anymore, Bobby," Kemp told him. "With all that money, you can just sit out here forever, and not be bothered about a thing."

Kemp stayed for a few more minutes, sitting quietly while they looked out at the ocean. But when Autry asked him how it was that he, a sheriff in the small town of Grape River, knew about the ultrasecret GalaxyNet, Kemp never replied. He just said it was time for him to go.

Autry saw him passionately kiss his wife goodbye

at the door. Then he overheard their hushed conversation:

She asked him: "All of it?"

"All of what?" Kemp asked back

"All of what you just told him. Is it true?"

"He's actually smiled today. I don't think I've ever seen him smile before."

"That doesn't answer my question," she said.

That's when Autry heard the man whisper back to her. "Is it all true or not? Let's just say that answer is top secret."

The next day

It was early afternoon when Autry woke up in his rocking chair.

He'd drifted off while he and his wife were doing a therapy session. She was reading him famous phrases and he had to remember who said them. He'd missed eleven in a row.

"I don't know," he said to her abruptly. "Maybe it was time for me to go. I mean, this last mess, how we didn't suspect the cargo ships all along . . . The only people who knew what was really up were those Coast Guard guys. They tried to tell us, I think. Or maybe not."

She just touched him lightly on the face. "I know a little about special ops," she said. "I learned a few things when we were first married. From what Agent Weir told me, you guys were the best. He wasn't trying to pull my leg. He wasn't trying to kiss up to me, or give you false praise. He said *you were the best*. And he would know."

She pulled his blanket up to his chin and kissed the top of his head. "I think it's time to go back to sleep . . ." she said.

Autry did. Rocking on the old chair, facing out to sea, the sun sinking slowly into the Pacific, she left him alone to dream some more.

WHEN HE OPENED HIS EYES NEXT HE SAW THAT THE sky had become filled with stars. The sun was gone, but its glow was still hanging on the horizon. A slight wind was blowing off the water.

He'd heard something strange. Far away, distant even, a low roar had awakened him. Coming out of nowhere, shaking everything around him, it was a noise that never sounded the same way twice, yet he had heard it a thousand times.

Now it was Autry's eyes that had tears in them. Naturally, he looked up to the heavens. And that's when he saw them.

Twelve twinkling lights, passing overhead, way up, but not so much that he couldn't see them among the stars.

It was them. XBat. Moving across the sky like ghosts. He just knew it.

He watched them for nearly a half hour, rocking slowly in his chair, until they disappeared over the horizon.

Then he just leaned back and smiled.

They looked like they had somewhere to go.